SPIRIT OF THE
HORSE

p

This is a Parragon Publishing Book

First published in 2005

Parragon Publishing
Queen Street House
4 Queen Street
Bath BA1 1HE, UK

Copyright © Parragon 2005

Designed, produced, and packaged by Stonecastle Graphics Limited

Photography by Bob Langrish
Text by Nicola Jane Swinney
Edited by Kate Green
Designed by Sue Pressley and Paul Turner

ISBN 1-40543-680-8

Printed in China

CONTENTS

HORSES ON FILM

The horse has been a part of our lives for many centuries and to capture the fitness, power, and agility of this most beautiful animal on film has been my passion for the last thirty years.

PHOTOGRAPHING THE horse at liberty, in the freedom of wide-open spaces, has often presented a challenge – from trying to get close to a group of nervous wild Mustangs by crawling (down-wind) on my hands and knees over rough terrain, to sitting patiently, coaxing a new-born foal out from behind its protective mother. But the key to success is to understand the horse's mind – the way it thinks and its strong natural instincts for survival.

Many times I have turned a stallion free in a pasture and it has only taken a few minutes to capture *the* single picture which shows him at his best; at a collected canter or an extended gallop which illustrates his strength and power, or at a floating trot where he will almost walk on air with all four hooves off the ground in a moment of suspended animation. The stallion will perform a pattern in his field, repeated many times until the initial excitement is replaced by curiosity. At this point it is possible to capture his character as he turns his attention on the photographer.

Often the photographer can attract his subject's attention by making different noises, including the sound of a "growling bear" when the horse may be surprised and turn as if to say: "What was that?". This is when he is likely to be at his most expressive.

Foals and groups of youngsters are always fun to photograph because they are naturally inquisitive, and it is possible to use their curiosity to achieve the perfect picture. If you scare a group of yearlings they will run away, bunch up together and walk back to you as a herd to check you out, ears forward and eyes popping out of their heads. Foals will always hide behind their mothers, but if the photographer sits quietly in the middle of a group he will soon have some close friends and great pictures.

At all times it is prudent to be aware of the instincts of the horse when entering its territory and to respect the way it thinks or you risk frightening it away or jeopardising your own safety by failing to understand its language of signals.

Photographing horses has taken me all over the world – to every continent, from the Russian herds in the Caucasus Mountains to the wild Mustangs of America. I have captured over 190 breeds with my camera, from the tiniest miniature horses to some of the largest horses in the world, and I have been privileged to photograph many of the world's most beautiful and valuable equines.

I hope you enjoy the images in this book and that they evoke something of the nature and spirit of this most magnificent animal – the horse.

Bob Langrish

SPIRIT OF THE HORSE

Why do I love horses? Well, what's not to love – how could anyone, looking at the sumptuous photographs in this book, fail to be rendered speechless with admiration and adoration?

IT IS difficult to imagine that there might be those who fail to be moved by these beautiful, generous, and intelligent creatures but indeed, my parents are among them. They couldn't understand my complete obsession with all things equine from the moment I realized that horses existed. Like many youngsters, I spent my entire childhood at the stables: grooming, mucking out, riding, or just inhaling that unmistakable sweet scent of horse. I think I probably drifted amid a miasma of "horse" for most of my formative years.

But the horse is so much more than a pet or a mere conveyance. Countless times I have heard owners say of their horse or pony, "he's such a nice person". If you don't own an equine, you would probably think they were being rather precious, but those who do will be nodding sagely – to them, the horse is a *person* with a strong individual personality.

While the horse has been an integral part of our lives for centuries, it is all too easy to forget that he is, essentially, a wild animal. We radically change the lives of our horses so that they can fit into ours.

But, thankfully, there are still herds of truly wild horses and it is a joy and a privilege to see them in their natural state; to watch them frolic and play, and kick up their heels with the sheer exuberance of living.

I remember, many years ago, we had a heavy snowfall one night in April and had to rush over to the stables to bring in the mares and their foals. It was four o'clock in the morning and icy cold; we were all somewhat befuddled with sleep and spent an hour chasing the youngsters around the field. The foals thought it a huge joke and would let us get just close enough to touch them with the headcollar before wheeling off again with boundless energy; racing and prancing – and snorting loudly into the freezing air. Just horses being horses.

In this book, you will find no pictures of horses being ridden nor in harness, just this most beautiful animal as he was meant to be – a free spirit. From the tiniest foal to the largest Shire, the unparalleled glory of the horse is showcased to perfection.

Of course everyone has their favorite, and I hope, within these pages, you will find yours. Will you be seduced by the cheeky charm of a little Welsh foal or will the Arabian's beauty win you over? Will you be enchanted by the majesty of the striking Andalucian or impressed by the magnificence of the Friesian, or, like me, will you find it impossible to single out just one? I hope you enjoy this book as much as I have enjoyed writing it and that, together with the stunning images, my words will convey something of the spirit of the horse.

Nicola Jane Swinney

Chapter 1
WILD HORSES

WILD HORSES

To the true horse lover, the realization that this magnificent creature, this powerhouse of bone and muscle, is essentially a wild animal only adds to his mystique.

WE ARE so accustomed to his domesticity – the riding school hacks, the docile ponies at summer fêtes – that to see the horse in his natural environment, whether it is the open plains of America, the Australian outback or the comparatively tame mountains and moorlands of the UK, brings us up short. We forget that he is part of our lives because of his nature, not just our coercion.

No other animal has lived so close to humans, nor captivated us for so long. From his early domestication, he has gone with us unquestioningly to war – and often perished – he became our foremost mode of transport, and is now our companion in competition and leisure. His destiny has always been linked with that of man. Yet swathes of our planet are still populated by wild horses, and how tragic it would be if that were to change. Where Darwin's law of survival of the fittest rules, the horse will continue to evolve and thrive and benefit man for years to come.

Naturally gregarious, horses are herd animals – any horse owner will know that horses turned out together in a field are likely to form a "pecking order", or hierarchy, and will, for the most part, remain as a group, even if they are of quite different types and breeds. Likewise, in the wild, horses

Above: *A powerfully built little horse, the Przewalski's diminutive stature belies his aggressive nature and his ability to survive in a harsh environment*

Above right: *Przewalski's Horse is said to be the last of the truly wild equines and, in 2003, a small herd was released back into the wild – for years, the only existing herds were in zoos*

> "The Przewalski is said to be the last of the truly wild horses or ponies."

Previous pages: *Przewalski's Horse provides the link between the "Dawn Horse" and today's modern breeds*

instinctively form herds, usually comprising several family groups of a stallion and perhaps five or six mares and their offspring. As a herd, they will sleep, play, and feed – a wild horse will graze for up to fourteen hours a day – while constantly being alert to any danger.

Although during the mating season stallions within the groups will fight for dominance over the breeding females, the herd is usually controlled by the older mares, who will keep in check any high spirits among the younger members of the herd, particularly the colts. But while domesticated stallions are generally perceived as more dominant and unpredictable than mares, the "matriarchs" of wild herds can be equally aggressive and far from submissive.

Safety for the wild horse is aided by a combination of excellent physical and sensory attributes – explosive speed and stamina to outrun any predator, as well as superb vision and hearing to detect any threat. For survival in the wild, the horse depends on the "fight or flight" mechanism. He has strong, protruding teeth and as a "weapon", particularly against another horse during a fight for supremacy, these can be formidable.

From a standing start, a horse can reach a top sprint

speed of forty-five miles per hour – about seventy kilometers per hour – in three or four seconds. His large eye, set either side of the head, has almost all-round vision, and his mobile ears, which can rotate almost through three hundred and sixty degrees, act like radar.

There is safety in numbers and a predator is likely be confused by a group of animals galloping around – an embarrassment of riches, rather than several separate meals. Here again, Darwin's theory comes into play: if a predator does manage to separate an animal from the herd, it is most likely to be old and weak or sickly, leaving the strongest, fittest members to survive and thrive. The herd's social structure, in which the co-operation of the group is combined with vigilance, ensures the safety of the individual. It also allows herd members to feed, play, and rest in comparative security.

Perhaps the most famous – not to say the most ancient – of the feral equines is Przewalski's Horse, or, more accurately, pony, since this rare breed stands between twelve and fourteen hands high (a hand equals four inches or 102mm). Named for Russian explorer Colonel Nikolai Mikhailovitch

the Tachin Schah – the "Mountains of the Yellow Horse" – west of the Gobi Desert, in 1879, these are said to be the last of the truly wild horses or ponies.

Also known as the Asiatic Wild Horse, he is an eerily primitive creature and, indeed, provides the link between the earliest known horses and the modern breeds. The breed differs from its domestic descendent in that it has sixty-six chromosomes instead of sixty-four. Despite his diminutive stature, he can be fierce and aggressive. A powerfully built animal, the Przewalski has had to adapt to a harsh existence in the Russian steppes and mountains of Mongolia, where poor vegetation and severe climate have honed his powers of endurance. He is believed to be migratory, moving north in the winter and returning to the south in the spring.

Charles Darwin believed that all domestic horses descended from "a single, buckskin-colored, more or less striped, primitive stock" to which the Przewalski, with his buckskin coloring, mealy muzzle, and eye markings, dorsal stripe, and "zebra bars" on his legs, would appear to bear witness.

In the summer of 2003, eight Przewalski's Horses, including in-foal mares, were released into Kazakhstan, where the breed had been extinct for some sixty years.

Above: *The wild Mustang of the United States of America is a real "melting pot", with little or no breed standard – they can be any color but are all hardy, with hard feet and a tough constitution*

Left: *The Mustang is thought to have roamed North America's great plains for around seven hundred years, having been been brought over to the New World by the Spanish explorers in the seventeenth century*

EARLY MORNING, misty dawn. Across the vast plains of the American West, nothing moves. Then an eagle, soaring high above the prairie, cries and a head lifts from a herd of horses that looked, until that moment, like a shadow. Another head, and another, eyes wide and ears pricked, and then, as one, the herd wheels about and gallops off, leaving nothing but dust and echo in its wake.

Anyone who has seen a Wild West movie, a US rodeo or even those Marlborough adverts will be familiar with the Mustang. These tough little horses populate much of the USA's great plains, and are thought to have done so for about seven hundred years.

The word Mustang derives from the Spanish *mestena* – "stray" or "ownerless" horse – and, indeed, the breed is thought to have evolved from horses brought over with Spanish explorers in the seventeenth century. Some of those horses escaped and took up residence in the wild, forming herds. They are notoriously shy and naturally fearful of people – hardly surprising given their treatment through the years. Yet like most equines, they can be tamed and are used as "cow ponies" – their speed and agility are renowned.

Above: *The Mustang comes in all colors, the most common being sorrel – a light chestnut shade – and bay, with skewbald, piebald, palomino, black, and grey also being seen*

Above right: *Early Mustangs were thought to be escaped Spanish imports who formed herds*

Horses were thought to be extinct in the US for more than ten thousand years before the arrival of the Spanish conquistadors, although horse fossils discovered in the United States show that the early equine ancestors were most certainly present.

The evolution of the horse is one of the best charted and most famous in all of science – the eventual decrease in the number of toes and the gradual increase in size; the early Eohippus or "Dawn Horse" was no bigger than a fox – and it is believed that an incredible nineteen species of equine inhabited the USA fifteen million years ago.

Hunted for their meat by both man and other predators, the horse population declined to extinction in the isolated continent until the arrival of the Spanish and their steeds, who were to change equine evolution beyond recognition.

These early imports were the Spanish Andalucian (chapter 3), Sorraia from Portugal, and Barbs from Morocco and, occasionally, a "throwback" to one of these distinctive breeds still appears in the wild herds. But for the most part, the Mustang is a stocky little horse standing barely more than 14hh, although height can vary from 13hh up to 16hh. Since his arrival in America, other breeds – such as the Morgan, Friesian, and Thoroughbred – have been added to the mix.

The melting pot that these wild herds have become means there is little or no breed standard; they come in all colors, all shapes and sizes, although they all possess hard feet, sound legs, and a tough constitution. The most common colors are sorrel, or light chestnut, with a flaxen mane and tail, and bay, but "paints" – skewbald or piebald – palomino and black are also seen.

"The evolution of the horse is one of the best charted and most famous in all of science."

With no selective breeding, by the nineteenth century the typical Mustang was likely to be coffin-headed, ewe-necked, roach-backed, and cow-hocked, in other words, possessing terrible conformation – hardly a romantic ideal of the wild horse!

But while he lacks the presence and power of the Andalucian or the lithe beauty of the Arabian, the Mustang is incredibly tough and hardy, with the ability to survive in the toughest terrain, and this was what saved him. At the beginning of the twentieth century, numbers of wild horses in the USA varied from an estimated one million to two million. But, hunted for their meat and culled to protect valuable grazing land for cattle, by the early 1970s there were less than twenty thousand left in the wild. "Mustanging", capturing and transporting wild horses for profit, became big business.

Above and previous page: *America's Mustang herds are now protected by the Wild Horse and Burro Act of 1971*

Above right: *Ever watchful, the wild Mustang has, in the past, been given all too many reasons to be nervous of man*

Right and far right: *These Mustang foals, watched over by their protective mothers, will need all their toughness to survive in the harsh conditions*

The capture and slaughter methods used were often brutal – the horses were rounded up by cowboys using trucks and helicopters and any that were injured could be left to die. The horse in North America appeared to be heading for a second extinction.

Largely thanks to the efforts of one woman, Velma Johnston – delightfully nicknamed "Wild Horse Annie" – who led a campaign of national publicity, a law was passed in 1959 to prohibit the use of aeroplanes and motorized vehicles to hunt wild horses and burros – small donkeys – on federally owned land. This was followed, to overwhelming public support, by the Wild Free-Roaming Horse and Burro Act of 1971, which designated the Mustang a protected species under the auspices of the Bureau of Land Management (BLM).

It is hard for any horse lover to imagine these wild creatures being slaughtered to be eaten. Who among us can picture a horse, any horse, and not imagine riding him – galloping him across an open field, or feeling the surge of power beneath as he bunches his muscles to clear a fence, a ditch or a stream? Romantics will have it that the Mustang is untameable, but this is not so. Far from being the mean-spirited rebel as he is oft portrayed, he is in fact quite biddable and can form strong bonds with humans.

It is thought that the Native American Indians were the first to tame the Mustang and he changed their lives. They were hunters of the mighty buffalo and, once they had mastered the art of riding the wild horses, they were no longer at a disadvantage. It could perhaps be argued that the taming of the Mustang contributed to the decrease of the buffalo population.

Above: *At one time, there were thought to be anything between one and two million Mustang, but their numbers decreased to an estimated twenty thousand left in the wild*

Left and far left: *Tough, agile and surprisingly fast, the Mustang became a valuable asset to the Native Americans and white settlers alike*

Above: *A stocky little horse, the Mustang retains many of the characteristics inherited from his Spanish forebears*

Right: *Members of a small herd drink at a watering station paid for by voluntary contributions*

To the Native Americans, the horse meant status and nobility. He was invaluable in war, he was currency and he could buy a bride – riches indeed. When a chieftain died, his horses were sacrificed to join him on the "other side".

But it wasn't long before the white man – the cowboys – discovered the Mustang as a means for transport rather than a substantial meal. The nimble little horse seems to possess an inherent "cattle sense" in that he is almost able to anticipate what a cow will do next, which secured his place as the cowboy's preferred mode of transport.

Today, this skill can be seen in Western riding competitions, where the Mustang excels. He is also used in rodeo and for pleasure riding. The Mustang remains a protected species and the Bureau of Land Management still monitors the herds. It even offers an adoption scheme to ensure the USA's wild horses continue to thrive.

"To the Native Americans, the horse meant status and nobility. He was invaluable in war, he was currency and he could buy a bride – riches indeed."

Left: *Although rarely standing more than 14hh, the wild ponies do bear some horse-like characteristics, hinting of their ancestry.*

Above and above right: *There is little nourishment on the marshland of Assateague, off the east coast, but the ponies of Assateague and Chincoteague are what is known as "good doers"*

"Highly intelligent and versatile, the Chincoteague makes a suitable mount for children, who love his merry nature and colorful markings."

Left: *A mare and foal display the typical skewbald markings of the wild herds, although solid colors do sometimes occur*

"BY MIDNIGHT, the swell had increased drastically and the moon was but briefly visible through the scudding clouds. The storm was whipping itself into a frenzy and waves slammed on to the decks. Barely, above the crashing water and shrieking wind, the horses could be heard screaming in terror."

Fiction? Well, perhaps. But a popular theory for the origins of the ponies on the island of Assateague, off the east coast of America, and its neighbor Chincoteague, a picturesque Virginian resort, is that the ponies swam ashore from a shipwrecked Spanish galleon.

More prosaically, it is likely the ponies are descendants of herds turned loose by early settlers, but they are still believed to have been of Spanish stock. Whichever, wild horses are thought to have inhabited these islands for some three hundred years, eking out an existence from the marsh.

They tend to be small in stature, standing an average of 12hh, but do exhibit some horse-like characteristics. Their existence did not become widely known until the 1920s and they now fall under the protection of the Chincoteague Fire Department, which manages both islands.

There are two herds on Assateague, which is unpopulated by people. The island is low-lying, with little protection from the Atlantic storms, and much of it is sandy marshland. There

is a saying that the Chincoteague pony "can get fat on a cement slab" – in other words, he is a "good doer".

Highly intelligent and versatile, he makes a suitable mount for children, who love his merry nature and colorful markings – most of the ponies are skewbald and piebald, although solid colors do occur. An infusion of Arabian blood has improved the quality of the herds.

Every July, the ponies are rounded up on Assateague and swum across to Chincoteague, where they are auctioned. Those unsold are swum back to their island the following day.

Above and right: *Wild horses are thought to have inhabited the islands for three hundred years, eking out an existence from the marsh*

"A popular theory for the origins of the ponies is that they swam ashore from a shipwrecked Spanish galleon."

Left: *It is said that this small hardy horse owes its size to the sparse vegetation available on the islands*

"The word Brumby is thought to have derived from the Aboriginal word baroomby, meaning wild."

HE IS often called Australia's national icon, yet the Brumby – the continent's only feral equine – has been, of all the wild breeds, perhaps the most persecuted.

Horses arrived in Australia with First Fleet in 1788, which brought English Thoroughbreds and Spanish horses. The long journey by sea was arduous and only the toughest survived – man and beast. Later, more Thoroughbreds were imported, along with Arabians and ponies. The Brumby, much like the American Mustang, descended from these early imports.

But in Australia, he is seen as a pest species, competing with cattle for food and water. The lack of selective breeding means many Brumbies are of poor quality and they are deemed by some to be too intractable to be used as riding horses. Indeed, the word Brumby is thought to have derived from the Aboriginal word, *baroomby*, meaning wild.

Because the feral herds adapted to the terrain and climate, they were prolific breeders and spread across the vast outback. They were hunted for their meat or shot to preserve pasture, and water supplies were fenced off.

Today, estimated numbers vary between three hundred and six hundred thousand. But in the summer of 2003, a further cull was in prospect – to stop them entering the Namadgi National Park in Canberra. The environment ministry said that if Brumbies had to be destroyed to keep them out, this must be done as "humanely" as possible.

Brumby Watch was lobbying to try to stop the cull and to preserve the feral horses of the Antipodes.

Above and right: *The Brumby is seen as a pest in Australia, competing with cattle for food and water in the harsh terrain*

Above: *The Camargue's thick white coat protects him from the cold winters and harsh winds of the region, a vast swampland in the Rhône delta*

Above right: *The wild ponies on the Camargue are known as "the white horses of the sea" and only about thirty herds currently exist*

Left: *There is little to nourish the Camargue horses, yet the herds thrive on the region's stunted grass and reeds – they will always manage to find something on which to feed*

THEY LOOK like ghosts; all grey, moving almost silently through the marsh in the early morning mist. Only the occasional whicker or a splash as they walk through the shallow water gives away their presence. These are the wild horses of the Camargue, a vast swampland in the Rhône delta in the south of France. There is little to nourish them here, where all that grows is stunted grass and reeds and where the mistral – the notoriously cold, strong north wind – howls across the delta.

Winters in the region are harsh, but these hardy creatures – known as "the white horses of the sea" – thrive and breed here. Their foals are born black, brown or dark grey, but they lighten with age; the older the pony, the lighter the color.

Their thick white winter coats offer excellent protection against the freezing temperatures suffered in the Camargue region – unless they get wet in heavy snow and quickly get cold. Fortunately, this is a rare occurrence.

There are only about thirty herds – or *manades* – comprising an estimated forty-five stallions and four hundred mares. In many places across the Camargue, the horses are maintained to improve the condition of the land; without the grazing herds, the land would be covered by shrubs and brambles and would become impenetrable and fallow.

Stallions are rare because, generally, they are captured and gelded (castrated) to be used as mounts. The chosen few remain entire, selected by the ranchers on the delta to produce future stock.

For two months of each year, starting in April, the selected stallion is allowed to run with a herd, of which he is lord indeed. If two stallions meet, a fierce and violent battle is almost inevitable. The stallion will mate several times with a mare who has come into heat, often watched curiously by the rest of the herd.

A mare will usually start bearing foals from her fourth year and, all being well, will continue for the next fifteen, giving birth each spring. Slow to mature and short in stature – the Camargue rarely exceeds 14hh – they are renowned for their longevity, living well past twenty-five years.

Although they have probably been indigenous to the region since prehistoric times – they bear strong resemblance to ancient cave drawings – the Camargue was only recognized as a breed in 1968.

They possess good bone and a hearty constitution. Their thick white coat offers excellent protection against the elements and their feet are generally hard and sound. They are no beauties, though; their heads are often coarse, necks short and the whole picture rather primitive.

But what they lack in looks they make up for in performance. Their active, high-stepping action makes them much prized by French cowboys – the *gardians* – who use them to drive the fierce black bulls of the area.

Now that some seventeen thousand acres of the Camargue is designated a national reserve, the white horse of the sea has a niche in the tourist industry – forming an integral part of this romantic landscape.

Right: *The horses of the Camargue actually help to maintain the land – without the grazing herds keeping the vegetation in check, vast areas would become impenetrable and the land would lie fallow*

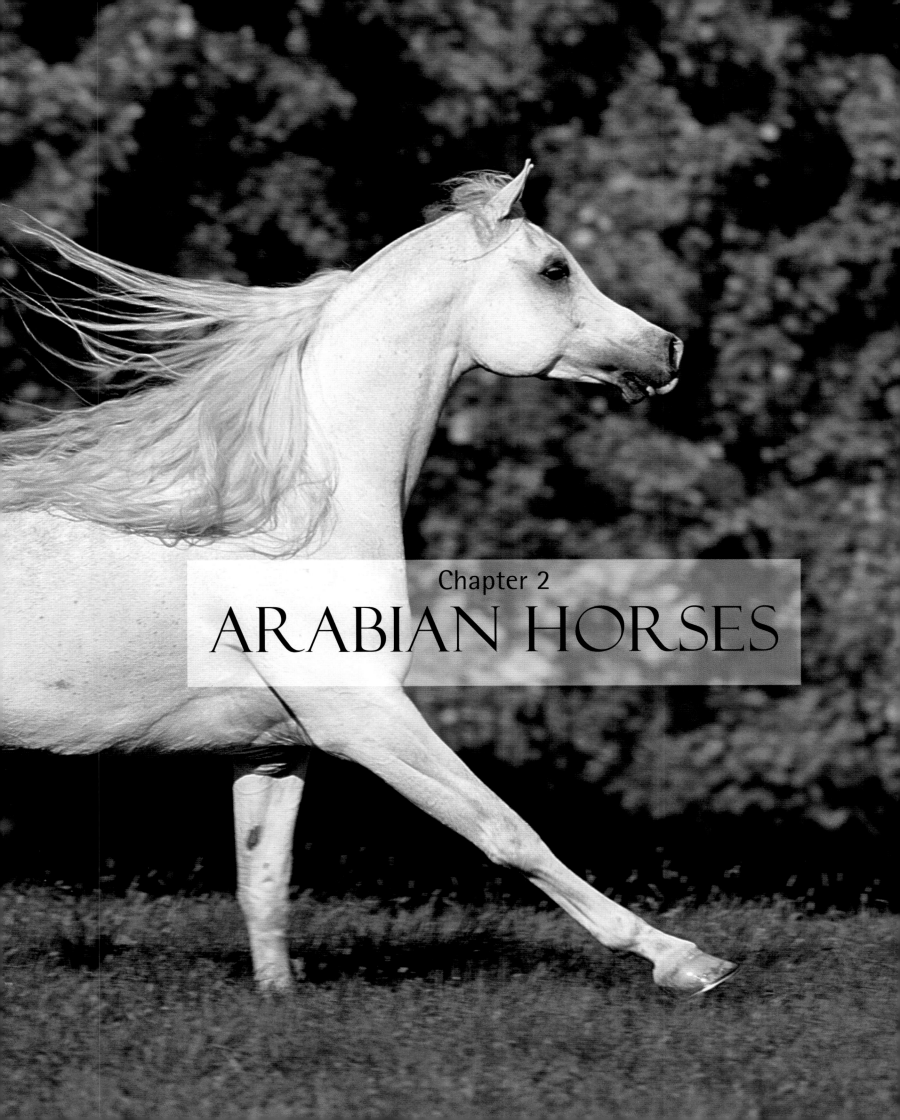

Chapter 2
ARABIAN HORSES

ARABIAN HORSES

*If any breed truly epitomizes the spirit of
the horse, it must surely be the Arabian.
This is the horse that every besotted little girl
draws – he looks like a fairy-tale.*

WITH HIS tiny, curved ears, large liquid eyes, extravagantly dished (concave) face and luxurious mane and tail, the Arabian is the horse of dreams.

The Arabian is undeniably beautiful and is the purest and possibly the oldest of all the breeds. The Arab people call him *keheilan*, meaning "pure blood, through and through". He has remained free of foreign blood and has maintained his distinctive – and stunning – breed characteristics.

One of the most notable differences between the Arabian and other breeds is the number of vertebrae: all other equine breeds have eighteen ribs, six lumbar vertebrae and eighteen tail bones; the Arabian has seventeen ribs, five lumbar vertebrae, and sixteen tail bones. He has another unique feature known as the *mitbah*, which is the angle where the head meets the neck. The Arabian's small head, with its tapering muzzle – his muzzle should fit into a half-cupped hand – is set high on his fine muscular neck. This results in an arching curve that allows the head to be incredibly mobile and to turn freely in almost any direction. Also unique to the breed is the *jibbah*, a shield-shaped bulge extending between

the Arabian's huge, wide-set eyes, upward to a point between the ears and down across the top third of the nasal bone.

His elegant neck sweeps gracefully to a rounded wither and strong, sloping shoulder, while his short back, with its high croup, is notably concave. He has a broad, deep chest encasing exceptionally strong lungs, which give the breed an ability to work unfailingly for considerable periods of time and make them ideal for endurance riding. Added to this are clean, hard legs – they are deceptively delicate, but Arabian bone is said to be denser than that of other breeds – and good, sound feet, which are almost perfect in shape.

Indeed, as much as he is prized for his beauty, the Arabian is revered for his speed and stamina, as well as his athleticism. His action is a joy to behold – he moves freely and lightly, as though on springs – as he appears to float. The long, silky mane and tail, which is carried exceptionally high, all contribute to the horse's enchanting appearance.

The Arabian is not a big horse, rarely exceeding about 15 hands high. The grey color – which, as with all breeds, lightens with age – adds to his fairy-tale charm, but all solid colors, except palomino, are seen. His coat is fine and silky, so the veining can be seen beneath, and has a high sheen, particularly in the chestnut and bright bay.

This beautiful ancient breed is thought to go as far back as 3000BC and has strongly influenced many of today's more modern breeds of horse.

Above: *It is easy to see the* jibbah, *the shield-shaped bulge between the wide-set eyes, on this typical grey Arabian*

Above left: *This stunning chestnut Arabian stallion has an almost metallic sheen on his fine and silky coat*

Previous pages: *This Arabian stallion epitomizes the fairy-tale quality of this unique and beautiful breed*

"His action is a joy to behold – he moves freely and lightly, as though on springs – as he appears to float."

It is said that when Allah created the horse, he said: "I call you Horse; I make you Arabian and I give you the chestnut color of the ant. I have hung happiness from your forelock which hangs between your eyes; you shall be the Lord of the other animals. Men will follow you wherever you go; you shall be as good for pursuit as for flight; riches shall be on your back and fortune shall come through your mediation." Then Allah put on the horse the mark of glory and happiness – a white star in the middle of the forehead.

In proclaiming that Allah had created the Arabian, the Prophet Mohammed believed that those who treated the horse well would be rewarded in the afterlife. This, coupled with the belief that "no evil spirit will dare to enter a tent where there is a pure-bred horse", encouraged further

breeding of the Arabian. As time went on, the Bedouin tribes of the Arabian deserts zealously protected and maintained the Arabian breed, striving to keep it *Asil* – or pure – in the form intended by Allah. Any mixture of foreign blood from the mountains or the cities surrounding the desert was strictly forbidden.

The Bedouins' highly selective breeding policies shaped the magnificent horse we see today, and who – through centuries of care and commitment – remains highly prized.

Because of the harsh desert conditions, the Arabian would work alongside and share food and water – and even, sometimes, accommodation – with his nomadic masters and, as a result, he developed a close affinity with man and high intelligence.

Much prized, the Arabian was primarily an instrument of war. A well-mounted Bedouin could storm an enemy settlement and capture the tribe's herds of camels, goats, and sheep, adding to his own tribe's wealth and, subsequently, to its status. Such a raid was extremely risky, and could only be achieved by taking advantage of both surprise and speed of the attack – and making good the escape.

The Arabian mare was deemed best for such forays, as she would not whicker to the enemy's horses, warning the tribe of the attackers' approach. These wonderful war mares exhibited great courage in battle, taking charges and spear attacks and giving no quarter. Speed and endurance – for which the Arabian is still famous today – were vital, as the raids were often carried out far from the tribe's own camp.

Above: *Note how far this Arabian's eyes are set apart, and his flaring nostrils*

Above left: *This Arabian illustrates the tiny, curved ears, dished or concave face, large liquid eye and small muzzle that typify the breed*

Far left: *This magnificent horse was bred by the Imperial Egyptian Stud in the USA – Egyptian lines remain highly prized, both in the US and in Europe*

The Arabian mare was thus beyond price. Mare families, or strains, were named according to the tribe or sheikh that bred them. Hence the five basic families of the breed were Kehilan, Seglawi, Abeyan, Hamdani, and Hadban. Although all combine the beauty and athleticism we associate with the Arabian, to the aficionado they are easily identifiable.

In all these major strains, the most common colors were grey, chestnut, and brown, or bay. Black was not a popular color, as it absorbs heat and a desert horse would not be as efficient with a black coat. Diligent breeders did their best to eliminate the color from their prized bloodlines. However, today most Arabians no longer live in the desert and black horses are becoming increasingly popular.

But each of these five distinct strains, when bred pure, developed recognisable characteristics, which made them readily identifiable. The Kehilan strain was noted for depth of chest, masculine power and size – the average height for Arabians of this strain was 15hh. Their heads were notably short and had an especially broad forehead, with exceptionally wide jawline.

Above: *All solid colors are permissible in the Arabian, apart from palomino, but black, like these mares, bred in California, is still relatively uncommon, although it is becoming more popular*

"The five basic families of the breed all combined the beauty and athleticism we associate with the Arabian."

Right: *This magnificent black stallion, bred in the UK, displays the legendary "mark of happiness and glory" – a white star – clearly on his forehead*

"The Bedouins' highly selective breeding policies shaped the magnificent horse we see today, and who remains highly prized."

Left: *Highly intelligent, the Arabian is alert to his surroundings*

Right: *Showing the spirit associated with the breed, this fine horse is clearly enjoying life*

Below: *Fast and agile, with a wiry athleticism, this mare lets off steam – note her beautiful flowing tail*

The Seglawi Arabian was particularly refined, possessing almost feminine grace and elegance. He had fine bone and stood only about 14.2hh, with a longer face and neck than the Kehilan. This sleek little horse, although perhaps lacking in stamina compared with his larger brothers, was renowned for his speed.

Similar to the Seglawi, the Abeyan strain was also refined, and pure-breds had longer backs than a typical Arabian. Like the beautiful Arabians shown here, the Seglawi was most commonly grey, with more white markings than other strains.

In contrast, the Hamdani horse could be considered plain – if that description could ever apply to the Arabian – with an athletic build and bigger bones. He lacked the pronounced *jibbah* and has a straighter profile and neck. He was a bigger model, standing at about 15.2hh.

The Hadban was a smaller version, standing under 15hh. Although he had a markedly muscular build and bigger bone, he was known for his gentle and tractable nature. The primary color was brown or bay, with very few, if any, white markings.

Substrains developed in each main strain, named after a celebrated mare or sheikh. But all had one thing in common

Top and above: *The Arabian's action is second to none – he appears to float, as if on invisible springs*

Left: *Although a roan color at present, this foal may well turn grey like his mother. Note her distinctive high tail carriage, a defining characteristic of the Arabian breed*

– they were bred in the desert, and evolved into the swift, graceful, and powerful mount of the Arab warrior. Possessing both speed and stamina, these remarkable horses were coveted by all who saw them and these superb steeds influenced the breeding of horses around the world.

It would be almost impossible to overestimate quite how influential these early Arabian horses were on the development of modern breeds. Horses were bred in Europe to carry a knight and his armor and lighter equines owed a lot to the pony breeds. The Europeans had nothing to compare with the swift, sleek horses of the Arab invaders. Rumors of the "Eastern" horse spread, with ever more fantastic tales of their speed, stamina and athleticism.

With the invention of firearms, the heavily armored knight became defunct, as did his weight-bearing charger; now cavalry was clamoring for lighter, faster and more nimble horses. Increasingly, wars proved the superiority of the Arabian and he became the mount of choice for the world's military. But it wasn't just the military who desired the horse of Arabia. To own such a horse carried increasing prestige, for this marvellous creature would improve local stock beyond measure. The Arabian became almost invaluable – Europeans of means, predominantly royalty, would go to almost any lengths to procure one.

A revolution was to take place in the history of horse breeding. For the Arabian – although regarded with scorn by

some factions of the modern horse world – played an enormous role in the development of the highly prized English Thoroughbred.

Three imported stallions formed the foundation of the Thoroughbred: The Byerley Turk, imported in 1683, The Darley Arabian in 1703 and The Godolphin Arabian in 1730. Ninety-three percent of all modern Thoroughbreds can be traced back to one of these three bloodlines on the male side.

The Byerley Turk was owned by Colonel Robert Byerley, who was thought to have captured him from a Turkish soldier in Budapest in the 1680s. Famously, the colonel took the horse – said to be a "particularly substantial Arabian" – to the Battle of the Boyne, where he escaped capture thanks to his steed's fleetness of foot.

Above: *"What are you looking at?" Curious, alert and intelligent, this baby is secure at his mother's side and shows no fear*

Above left: *Mirror image – how similar are this mare and her foal, pictured at an Arabian stud in California; they both show the same proud head carriage*

"The Arabian mare was beyond price and mare families, or strains, were named according to the tribe or sheikh that bred them."

Left: *This lovely mare shows the fluid action of the breed, while her enchanting chestnut foal has a pronounced dished face*

"The Arabian played an enormous role in the development of today's highly prized English Thoroughbred."

Left: *The beauty of the Arabian is unsurpassed and he was to become almost invaluable in improving existing stock*

Right: *The Arabian possesses speed, strength, stamina and soundness, all of which benefited the Thoroughbred*

Above: *This Arabian stallion has all the spirit and fire found in the breed, which also has an exceptionally gentle and tractable nature*

Left: *Arabian mares turned out at an American stud come to see what is going on – their interest and curiosity are an indication of the high intelligence possessed by the breed*

The Byerley Turk was retired to stud around 1690, standing first at Middleridge Grange in County Durham and then at Goldsborough in Yorkshire. The horse is said to have stood at stud for some eleven years, so he obviously possessed stamina as well as speed.

Also standing at stud in the north of England, The Darley Arabian sired perhaps the greatest racehorse of all time, Flying Childers, who was unbeaten in all his eighteen races. The Darley Arabian was acquired by Thomas Darley, British consul in what was then Syria, and was described as "a horse of exquisite beauty". He stood at the Yorkshire stud belonging to Darley's brother. Little is known about the third stallion, The Godolphin Arabian, although he is thought to have been born in the Yemen and brought to England by Edward Coke of Derbyshire. Edward Coke, a renowned livestock breeder of the day, discovered the stallion as a five-year-old pulling a coal cart through the streets of Paris, although this may be apocryphal. Coke later sold him to Lord Godolphin.

But the influence of the Arabian does not stop at the English Thoroughbred. His bloodlines enriched and enhanced such diverse breeds as the Welsh Mountain pony, whose dished face and neat muzzle are reminiscent of more exotic ancestry; the Austrian Haflinger and his Italian counterpart, the Avelignese, trace back to the Arabian stallion, El Bedavi, and the Orlov Trotter, an eighteenth century carriage horse developed in Russia, originated from an Arabian cross. The Lipizzaner's exclusive grey color is owed to Arabian blood, while the Morgan horse of America is thought to have been of predominantly Arabian and Thoroughbred ancestry.

Indeed, the part the Arabian has played in the development and refinement of other horse breeds throughout the world is unmatched.

It has been said of the Arabian: "It is the oldest bloodstock of all; it is a tap root, not a derivation from anything else at all. It has the gift, possessed alone by true root stock, of absolute dominance in breeding and unrivalled power of impressing its own character on any other breed with irresistible force. The Arabian is the chief and noblest origin of our national racehorse, of the best breeds of North Africa, and of light horses all over the world."

Today, there are still distinct Arabian strains and types. Perhaps the most famous line is that of the Crabbet Stud, founded in Britain before the turn of the nineteenth century by Lady Anne and Sir Wilfred Scawen Blunt, who bought horses from the desert Bedouins and imported them from

Above: *This glowing creature illustrates the striking characteristics of her breed*

Right: *A perfect demonstration of the "floating action" with tail held high*

1878 onward. One of the most important was a mare, Rodania, and the stallions Mahruss II and Mesaoud. Crabbet lines, though increasingly rare, are highly valued and the description can only be applied to Arabians descended from lines owned by the Blunts.

The Egyptian Arabian, too, is greatly prized, being descended from the herds of Mohammed Ali Pasha and his grandson Abbas Pasha, as well as twenty horses from Crabbet sent to Lady Blunt's Sheikh Obeyd Stud in Egypt. President Nasser of Egypt subsequently gave a stallion, Aswan, to the Tersk Stud in Russia, where he was widely used on racing lines and mares of Polish breeding. Polish Arabs are known for their substance and beauty.

The Persian Arabian – though similar to his better-known counterpart – is thought to be older by some fifteen hundred years, although numbers are now greatly reduced. Very much alike in characteristics and conformation, he is slightly stockier but possesses great presence and bearing.

In Hungary, the Shagya Arab was developed in the eighteenth century. The country's oldest stud, Mezőhegyes, was founded in 1785, but the Babolna Stud, founded in 1789, is now famous for its Arabian horses. The Shagya is a practical horse with more bone than the Arabian, and is predominantly grey in color, although he is named after a cream stallion on which the breed was founded. The stallion was big for an Arabian, standing just over 15.2hh, and gave

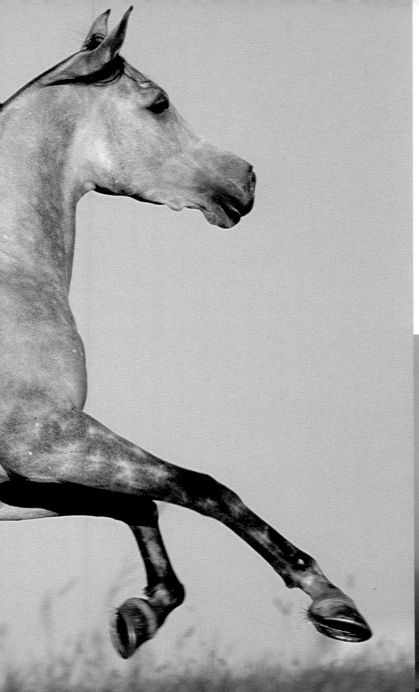

Following pages: *The Arabian horse has had an almost unquantifiable influence on the world's modern breeds*

Left: *This fine stallion was bred at the Imperial Egyptian Stud*

Below: *The pure-bred Arabian will continue to be revered for his great beauty*

the Shagya breed its substance. In France the emphasis is on racing and so French Arabians have been bred to resemble the Thoroughbred more closely than their English counterparts. Australia has also produced some superb Arabians, whose strong limbs and hard feet allow them to excel at endurance riding.

The USA is a comparatively young nation in terms of horse culture, but it has the distinction of having the largest population of pure-bred Arabians in the world. Throughout the world, the Arabian horse has made his mark. Revered for his purity, diligent breeding keeps those exalted bloodlines undiluted. And his enduring beauty means he will be in demand for centuries to come.

"The part the Arabian has played in the development and refinement of other horse breeds throughout the world is unmatched."

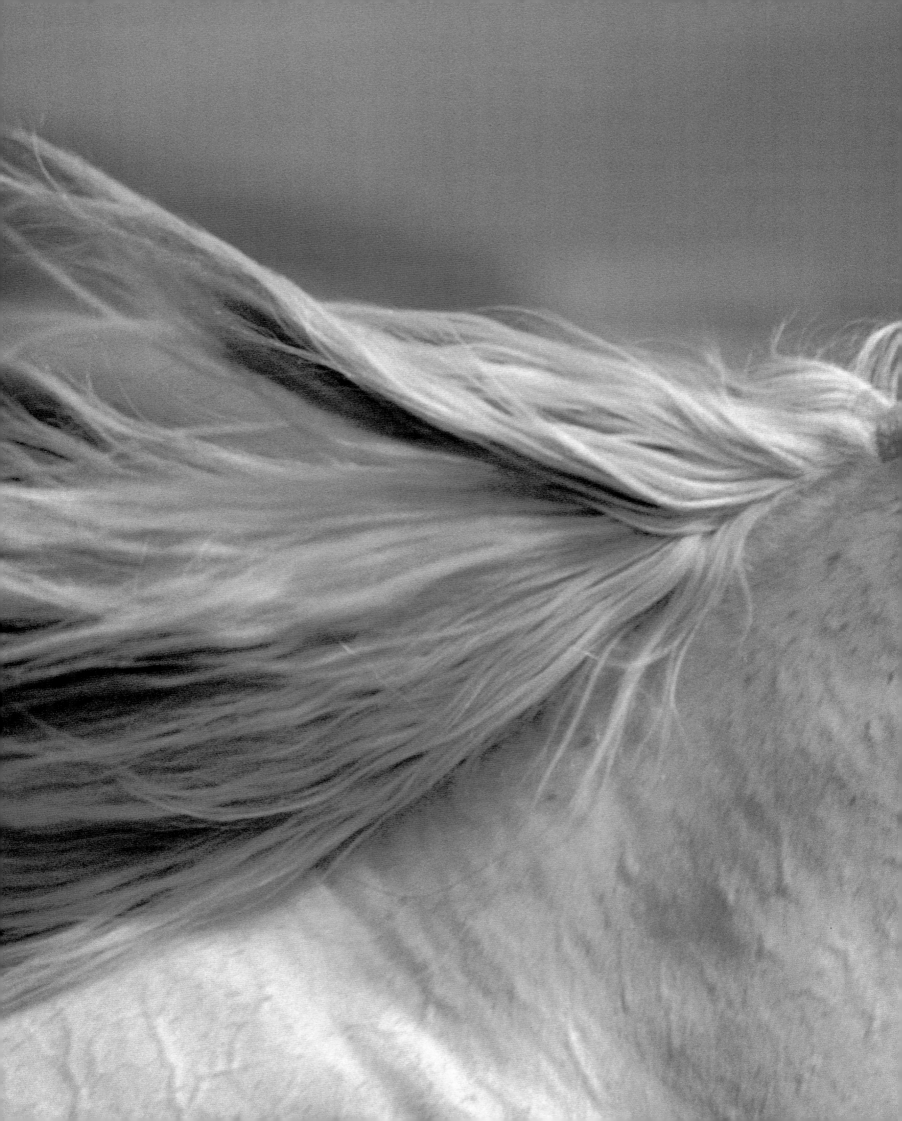

Chapter 3

IBERIAN HORSES

IBERIAN HORSES

*Iberia's "noble kings", the Andalucian and Lusitano,
are horses of great beauty, prized for their flamboyant
high-stepping action. In terms of equine development,
the horses of Spain are second only to the Arabian.*

CLINGING TO the edge of the hillside, the white village glows against the cobalt sky, the afternoon sunshine glinting off the turquoise water in backyard swimming pools. An air of barely contained excitement hangs over the little town, as mothers thread their daughters' hair with flowers and flamenco music leaps and cavorts from every square.

Hooves clattering on the cobbles, the muscular grey stallions toss their heads and bunch their powerful quarters, already infected with the exuberance of the growing crowd. Their long, rippling manes and tails are decorated with brightly colored ribbons and their arched necks are garlanded with flowers. These are the horses of Andalucia, the southern region of the Spanish mainland, and as much a part of the area's famous festival as the rhythmic snap of castanets and seductive strumming of the guitar. These Iberian kings are proud indeed; their history is long and noble and their influence on equine development, both ancient and modern, almost impossible to quantify.

Cave drawings found close to what is now Malaga on Spain's modern Costa del Sol, which date back to about 5000BC, depict a close approximation to the Spanish horse of today. In terms of equine evolution, the Andalucian – and, by association, his Portuguese cousin, the Lusitano (pictured right) – plays a major role, close on the heels of the Arabian (chapter 2) and what is thought to be his direct ancestor, the Barb. Indeed, it has been mooted that the Andalucian developed from Przewalski's Horse – or Asiatic Wild Horse – (chapter 1), or from the ancient steppe horse that is believed to have roamed the region from the Atlas Mountains and Spanish sierras to Turkmenistan. But most would agree that these horses trace back at least to the Moorish occupation of Spain in the eighth century, when the conquering invaders mixed the indigenous equines with their Barb horses. The Andalucian and Lusitano are but two names for these magnificent horses, which may also be referred to variously as Carthusian, Alter-Real, Peninsular or Zapatero. In order to avoid more confusion, they are perhaps best summed up as the Pura Raza Española – the pure-bred Spanish horse – or the Iberian horse.

The pure-bred Spanish horse was unified as a breed in the sixteenth century – between 1567 and 1593 – by King Philip II of Spain, who formally established the standards for the breed which is recognized today. The Andalucian name comes from the sun-drenched region of southern Spain encompassing Seville, Jerez, Cordoba and Granada, but for centuries the term Andalus referred to the entire peninsula. But the pure-bred Spanish horse still owes much to modern Andalucia, for it was thanks to an order of Carthusian monks that the breed remains pure to this day. Founded in 1476 at Jerez de la Frontera, near the coast, the Monastery of Cartuja kept a small herd of Spanish horses and preserved only the purest strains. The hot and dry climate of this area played its part in developing a breed with the hard, sound feet, and fine body hair that are his defining characteristics.

Renowned as an outstanding cavalry horse from the time of the ancient Greeks – whence the renowned general Xenophon, historian and philosopher, first established the art of horsemanship as we now know it – they were prized for their flamboyant high-stepping gait and extreme agility. Fearless and beautiful, these were the warhorses of kings.

Writing in the sixteenth century, Salomon de la Broue (1530-1610), riding master for King Henry IV, opined: "I class the true Spanish horse as the greatest. . . the most handsome, the most noble, the bravest, and most worthy of kings."

Left and above: *Beautiful and fearless, the Andalucian was prized as a warhorse*

Previous page: *A handsome Lusitano stallion has all the breed's nobility*

Yet the breed description does little to convey the Spanish horse's beauty and tremendous presence. The Andalucians pictured on these pages are the typical grey of the breed, although bay, roan, and black are also seen. It is said that, of the modern Andalucian, some eighty percent are grey, fifteen percent bay, and five percent black, although these are general estimates.

He stands about 15.2hh and is compact and short-coupled, with a sloping croup (hindquarters) and low-set tail. He is known to be intelligent and his noble profile is convex – rather than concave like that of the Arabian – and rather hawk-like, with a broad forehead. His classically beautiful head is instantly identifiable. History can be read deep in his large oval eyes, set inside a triangular orbital arch and the

"I class the true Spanish horse as the greatest…the most handsome, the most noble, the bravest, and most worthy of kings."

flare of his inverted, comma-shaped nostrils hint at the strength needed for extended effort. The shape and dexterity of his upper lip are pronounced; his mouth is highly sensitive and mobile. He has a muscular, crested neck that sweeps into a long, sloping shoulder and his deep body is balanced by powerful rounded quarters. His spectacular mane and tail are typically luxuriant and often wavy. His clean legs have plenty of bone and his action is nothing less than spectacular. It is this proud action that sealed the future of the Iberian horse and for which he is famed.

It is said that when King Philip II unified the pure-bred Spanish horse, he did so to bring to life the universally idealized equine that figured so large in historical pictorials, in sculpture and in art. He selected from the basic horses bred at the time in Spain those which came closest to this ideal and instructed that only these idealized horses should be used for his breeding program.

Horses of recognisably Spanish origins are still seen depicted in equestrian art and echoed in important sculpture – the mounted statue of King Charles I in London's Trafalgar Square is a prime example. Long coveted as the horse of the military – the Andalucian is said to be as brave and biddable as he is pleasing to the eye – with the invention of firearms in the fifteen century, the agile Spanish pure-bred was even further in demand.

The horse has a notably high degree of flexion in his hindlegs, which means he moves naturally in collection – and this agility remains highly prized and has played a part in the Spanish pure-bred's influence on other breeds.

As well as being bred as a warhorse, the Iberian breed was developed for working the lithe black bulls destined for the Spanish bull-ring and he is still used to fight in Spain's traditional arenas to this day. He is not built for galloping, but is incredibly supple and quick on his feet. He can turn on the proverbial dime yet, for all his fiery presence, he is gentle and docile. It is this inherently and uniformly sensible temperament that is invaluable to the *rejoneadores* – the mounted bull-fighters – who use exclusively the pure Spanish horse. While the bull-fight, which is perhaps abhorrent to some, is the domain of the Spanish, their spectacular horses are greatly prized worldwide. Although their distinctive high-stepping action – known as the gait *paso de andatura* – can work against them in the dressage arena, their athleticism is particularly suited to the movements of high school, or the *Haute École*.

Above: *The Andalucian has a muscular, crested neck with a spectacular mane and tail which are typically luxuriant*

Add the Lusitano – like this mare and her foal (above) – to the mix of the Pura Raza Española and the picture gets even more confusing. Compare the Lusitano above with the Andalucian and her foal (right), and there appears little to choose between them. The Lusitano is called after the old name for Portugal, Lusitania, and although he undoubtedly has an Andalucian base, he has developed a little differently.

At a maximum of 16hh, he stands a little taller than his Spanish cousin and is what is called more "on the leg" – that is, there is more daylight between his body and the ground.

Above: *A Lusitano mare and foal; the name comes from the old term for Portugal, Lusitania*

Right: *An Andalucian mare and foal, which stand slightly smaller than their Portuguese cousins*

Previous pages: *Lusitano youngstock*

The Lusitano, like the Andalucian, is thought to date back to a more primitive ancestor, the Sorraia, a pony that was probably a descendant of the Asiatic Wild Horse (chapter 1) and the Tarpan, which it closely resembles. There remains considerable confusion about the Tarpan – the name literally translates as "wild horse" – an Eastern European breed, but he is generally considered to be closer genetically to the modern horse than the Asiatic Wild Horse.

The Sorraia, and the closely related Garrano of Portugal, has contributed directly to the evolution of the Spanish horse. This primitive Iberian breed was influenced by North African stock, due to the land bridge that joined Spain to the "Dark Continent" before the last Ice Age, thousands upon thousands of years ago. The buckskin color occasionally thrown up in the Lusitano possibly traces back to the little Sorraia.

The pony breed, whose name – comparatively recently coined – derives from the Rivers Sor and Raia, which run through both Spain and Portugal, still exists today. Like many breeds, he has benefited from an out-cross to Arabian blood and is now very much a miniature Iberian horse, a scaled down version of the Andalucian or the Lusitano. The modern Sorraia rarely exceeds 13hh and has a large head with the typically primitive convex profile. He is an incredibly tough and hardy pony, able to resist extremes of temperature and to thrive on sparse forage.

It could be argued that the Lusitano – whose name is also relatively new, having only been in usage since 1966 – is even more "pure" than the Andalucian, whose infusion of Arabian blood can be seen in his more oriental head. That is not to say the Lusitano, with his large, kind eye, and neat, curving ears, is not as good-looking a horse as his Spanish cousin. His pronounced Roman nose and wide forehead is set on a short, thick neck upon powerful and quite upright shoulders. He has a broad chest, with plenty of heart room; a short, compact back with well-sprung ribs, muscular quarters, and long, strong legs. And, typical in the pure-bred Spanish horse, he possesses the same abundant, rippling mane and tail as the Andalucian.

Above right: *This herd of Lusitano mares are content and relaxed in their summer meadow*

Right: *In their shaggier winter coats, this happy herd of Lusitanos appear almost stocky, almost ponyish*

The Lusitano perhaps lacks some of the natural presence of the Andalucian, but is just as athletic and hence was equally prized as a cavalry horse and as a bull-fighter. One thing he certainly doesn't lack is speed and his elevated action and natural athleticism come into their own in the Portuguese bull-ring.

The Portuguese bull-fight is conducted entirely on horseback, so the horses must be highly schooled to swerve in an instant. It is considered a great disgrace for the *rejoneadores* if a horse is injured during the fight.

Imagine the courage it takes to face down an enraged and charging bull. As any event rider will agree, a faint-hearted horse is a dangerous horse. The Lusitano is renowned for his courage and is intelligent and responsive, traits that make him suited to the *Haute École*.

As can be seen from these three Lusitanos (above), again like the Spanish equivalent, the horses' color, although predominantly grey, can also be black, bay or chestnut. Buckskin is also – though rarely – seen, as is a striking mulberry shade.

It is thought the Lusitano was developed from the Andalucian by using more Arab blood, although – as can also been seen in the grey pictured above – there is little evidence of this in the horse's tail carriage, which is noticeably lower than that of the Andalucian, and his croup is usually more sloped. As illustrated above, the convexity of the head is more pronounced in the Lusitano.

Above: *Lusitano yearlings display the wider range of colors in the breed*

Above left: *The Lusitano tends to be more solidly built than the Andalucian*

Both the Lusitano and the Andalucian are becoming increasingly popular in the USA The Spanish horse is thought to have first arrived in the States in the cargo holds of the conquistadors, beginning with the second voyage of Christopher Columbus.

The breed made its second official appearance in the USA as late as the 1960s, but although the importation process was slow and costly, the horses of Spain found a vast fan-base in the States, where their beauty is revered. Their elasticity makes them highly adaptable and they are used for Western pleasure and trail riding, as well as the Olympic disciplines such as dressage – at which they excel – and show jumping.

"The perfect bond
between Iberian man and
horse may have provided
the original inspiration
behind the legend of
the centaurs."

Right: *The Andalucian is said to be as
brave and as biddable as he is pleasing
to the eye*

Right: *These Andalucians display the exuberant and elastic paces for which the breed is renowned*

"A horse of enormous presence, he was in great demand as a cavalry mount."

Below: *This impressive Andalucian stallion is a fine example of his breed*

It is easy to see why the Andalucian is so in demand; the horses on these pages – all pictured in Texas – show beautifully the energetic and elastic paces for which the breed is renowned. An active horse of enormous presence, he was in great demand as a cavalry mount, before his strength and courage were found to be invaluable in the bull-ring and on the farms where the bulls are worked. The Andalucian is also used in a discipline that is distinctly Spanish, called the *doma vaquera*, a formalized show ring version of farm work, most closely related to a reining pattern with combined dressage elements.

However, the Spanish horse almost became a victim of his own success. He was seen as a "specialist's mount" and, as

riding became less of an academic endeavor and more of a popular sport in the nineteenth century, classical equitation declined and, with it, the Andalucian. He became almost a horse of folklore. In his book *Cavalo Lusitano o Filho do Vento*, Arsénio Raposo Cordeiro wrote: "The perfect bond between Iberian man and horse may have provided the original inspiration behind the legend of the centaurs, a hybrid man-horse creature deemed to spring from the valleys of the Tagus River."

Soon, it was only the great traditional families who continued to keep the Andalucian. But among these families was the Domecq dynasty – one of the great sherry producers of the region – which owned some 38,000 acres of land in

the area. And in 1972, Don Alvara Domecq, the first *rejoneador* of Spain, founded the Royal Andalucian School of Equestrian Art, which was to gain worldwide renown. Situated in the heart of Jerez, the Royal School has seating for up to sixteen hundred spectators who flock every week to see the famous equestrian ballet, *Como Bailan Los Caballos Andaluces* – or "How Andalucian Horses Dance".

The academy is famed for equestrian excellence and trains riders of high standing, many of whom excel in more traditional dressage, such as Rafael Soto, who was seventh in the 1996 Atlanta Olympics, and Ignacio Rambla, while several of their horses have featured in medal-winning teams including at the 2002 World Equestrian Games in Jerez.

Above: *The energetic paces of the pure-bred Spanish horse make him ideal for the movements of the high school*

"The Spanish horse's strength and agility, his nobility and grace, his power and his beauty, make him a perfect dancer."

Left: *The classically beautiful head of the Lusitano*

Portugal, too, has its own School of Equestrian Art, which uses mostly the Alter-Real, a classical high school horse that has benefited from infusions of Andalucian blood. The Spanish horse's strength and agility, his nobility and grace, his power and his beauty, make him a perfect "dancer", and his influence stretches to those most famed of "balletic" horses, the dancing white stallions of Vienna.

Lipizzaners (chapter 4), which are used exclusively by the world-famous Spanish Riding School of Vienna, like many horse breeds in Europe and the Americas, descend directly from the Andalucian. Spanish horses taken to Lipica – or Lipizza – in 1583 were the foundation of the Lipizzaner breed and the name of the school pays homage still to its "Spanish" roots. It is the Spanish breed's versatility and biddability that contributed to the Lipizzaner's ability to dance. And anyone who has been lucky enough to visit the Spanish Riding School of Vienna will have seen how those wonderful white stallions really do dance.

Left and far left: *The Andalucian's luxuriant mane and tail are typically wavy*

"Spanish horses were to become the foundation stock of the many and varied equine breeds of today."

Below: *The Andalucian has a classically beautiful head which is instantly identifiable*

Above: *The proud and almost aristocratic demeanor of the Andalucian is a strong feature of the breed*

Left: *This Andalucian has the luxuriant wavy mane typical of the breed*

Right: *This magnificent bay Andalucian stands in Texas – Spanish horses were brought to the US by the conquistadors*

With so much history resting on his shoulders, it is fitting that the Iberian horse has such aristocratic bearing, exquisitely portrayed by this splendid Lusitano stallion (below), whose proud heritage is written all over him. And he and his Spanish counterpart (right) have, between them, played an almost unquantifiable part in the evolution of the world's horse and pony breeds.

During the sixteenth and seventeenth centuries, Andalucians were transported by Christopher Columbus and the conquistadors to the New World, the Americas, where horses had been extinct for thousands of years. These Spanish imports were to become the foundation stock of the many and varied equine breeds that today flourish across the USA – the Mustang, Criollo, Paso Fino and the distinctive spotted Appaloosa.

Right: *Andalucians like this stallion have played a major role in the evolution of the world's horse and pony breeds*

Below: *This Lusitano stallion has all the breed's beauty and nobility*

The American Quarter Horse, too, a compact and speedy little equine, is thought to have descended from Spanish horses crossed with English stallions. He is notably agile – being used for working cattle and Western pleasure riding – which he perhaps owes to his Spanish forebears. Great Britain's own celebrated native ponies, including the Irish Connemara and the Welsh Cob, and the Cleveland Bay horse which is noted for his excellent bone, all owe much to Spanish blood.

The Friesian horse of the northern Netherlands is almost an Iberian "in negative" – here is the Andalucian's noble head; compact, strong body; sloping quarters and sturdy legs; long, rippling mane and tail, but the Friesian is always black. Spanish stock also contributed to the Kladruber, when Emperor Maximilian II founded a stud at Kladruby in Bohemia – which was to become part of the Czech Rebublic – in 1572. This magnificent horse is an Andalucian on a much larger scale; predominantly grey, he originally stood at around 18hh, but has since become smaller and more active.

The little-known Frederiksborg and his striking spotted cousin, the Knabstrup, have Spanish ancestry, too – the former being named for King Frederik II of Denmark who founded the Royal Frederiksborg Stud in 1562. The Frederiksborg was developed as a charger for the Danish military that could also be used in the riding school, in parades and in court ceremonies.

He was an elegant and spirited horse, usually chestnut, with a showy, high-stepping action. But for all this he had a tranquil and agreeable temperament, like his Spanish ancestors. The Knabstrup dates from the Napoleonic wars, during which Spanish soldiers were stationed in Denmark. They brought with them spotted horses, which were often evident in early Spanish stock.

These ancient Iberian breeds have such history and lineage that they have featured in many ancient writings. Homer refers to them in the *Iliad* around 1100BC and Xenophon had nothing but praise for "the gifted Iberian horses and horsemen".

A horse named Babieca was the mount of Spain's "national hero" Ruy Diaz – immortalized on the silver screen as *El Cid* – for more than twenty years. Babieca died at the age of forty and was buried at the monastry of San Pedro de Cardena, where a memorial stands in his honor.

These proud horses are rare – it is thought that there are as few as five thousand breeding Lusitano mares worldwide and there are thought to be only about twelve thousand five hundred Andalucians left in Spain today. But their beauty and presence ensure those revered bloodlines will be guarded jealously and cherished for years to come.

Above: *The beauty and presence of the Iberian horse are undeniable*

Right: *Many of the world's most popular horse and pony breeds owe some of their characteristics to Spanish foundation stock*

Chapter 4
HORSES OF EUROPE

HORSES OF EUROPE

*The demise of the cavalry mount and the rise
of the competition, or leisure, horse has led to
the refinement of European horses, who now
dominate the Olympic disciplines.*

IF YOU look at almost any European horse breed, it is likely, somewhere, that you will find at least a trace of the Arabian (chapter 2). There is no greater an example of this than the English Thoroughbred who – revered throughout the world for his turn of foot, his stamina and his beauty – is directly descended from the Arabian.

This racing machine, this eleven hundred pounds (five hundred kilos) of bone and muscle, can sprint at speeds of more than forty-five miles (seventy-two kilometers) per hour and can jump a distance, lengthwise, of some thirty feet (nine meters). He is bred to race and will race like the wind,

using all his might to be the one who gets his head first past the post. But he is not just glorying in his fantastic power; his yearning and determination to be first is bred into him, an echo of his herding history and "fight or flight" instinct. First is strongest, mightiest, and best. First is supreme.

Of all the world's breeds, the Thoroughbred is the fastest and the most valuable, and on his back rests a multi-billion dollar racing and breeding industry. The racecourses of Britain, the USA, Japan, Australia, New Zealand and France echo with the resonating thunder of his hoofbeats and the names of exceptional horses reverberate down through the

Previous pages, below and right: The Thoroughbred may be any solid color, except palomino, with white markings, although the most common colors are variations of brown, chestnut and bay. Grey Thoroughbreds owe their color to their Arabian forebears

centuries. Britain has a long history of "running horses", and there were already several racecourses in existence before King James I set up the race track at Newmarket in the seventeenth century.

It is said that Richard the Lionheart devised the first race – for which he donated three prizes – on Epsom Moor. The native stock of running horses was probably created by mixing Spanish, Neopolitan, and Barb blood with the Irish Hobby – an antecedent of the Connemara pony – and the Scottish Galloway, as well as other native breeds. But, as throughout history, man wanted better, faster, stronger, and so the monarchy and nobility who were the participants in racing sought to find a breed designed primarily for speed.

There was a vital element missing in these early racehorses – Arabian blood. With the introduction of the three foundation stallions, The Byerley Turk, The Darley Arabian, and The Godolphin Arabian, in the late eighteenth century, the English Thoroughbred was born. Indeed, the name Thoroughbred is a literal translation of the word *kehilan*, meaning pure-bred.

The Darley Arabian sired Flying Childers, who in turn sired superb stock. His great-great-nephew, Eclipse, was perhaps the most famous racehorse of all time. He was unbeaten in all eighteen of his races and went on to sire an estimated three hundred winners. Diomed was exported to America where he went on to sire a dynasty, and the American Stud Book was first published in 1873.

With these three foundation sires – and something like ninety-three percent of all modern Thoroughbreds can trace back to one of them – came the beginning of the fantastic speed merchant we know today. Flying Childers, Herod, Eclipse, Diomed – who won the first ever Derby in 1780 – and Matchem, and more lately, Mill Reef, Arkle, and Sadler's Wells, ensured that England had the world's finest horses. The three original new bloodlines brought beauty and refinement and an enduring trait in the modern Thoroughbred – courage.

Today's racehorse is a horse of great beauty and presence, which he owes to his Arabian inheritance. Standing on average 16hh, he has a fine, lean head with a straight profile – unlike his concave-faced ancestors – with big, expressive eyes and large nostrils.

Thoroughbreds are raced at two years old, by which time their limbs may not be fully developed, but their long legs are clean and powerful, producing the racehorse's glorious sweeping stride.

"Ninety-three percent of all modern Thoroughbreds can be traced back to three foundation sires."

First records of the English Thoroughbred were published in 1791, entitled *An Introduction to a General Stud Book*, with volume one of the *General Stud Book* following in 1808. The existence of this first "introduction" was due to one James Weatherby, who painstakingly researched pedigree lines, and Weatherbys continues to keep records of Thoroughbred racehorses today. A horse can only race in Britain if he is registered with Weatherbys, and he can only be registered with Weatherbys if he is a Thoroughbred. His name can only be registered if it contains eighteen characters – including spaces and any punctuation – or less, and is not offensive in any way, although this last criterion has been occasionally and memorably breached.

Early Thoroughbreds were probably smaller than today's racehorses, although they were bigger than the pony racers who were competed over four miles. By now called

Thoroughbreds, the horse was bred to be bigger and faster over shorter distances – breeders wanted quicker returns on their investments, so races were shortened and the weights used to "handicap" the runners reduced. Because the Thoroughbred no longer had to be kept hardy enough to race over the four-mile track, they could be kept inside and fed, producing bigger horses that matured earlier. Thus the stock grew finer and taller – between the eighteenth and nineteenth centuries the Thoroughbred became one and a half hands (six inches) taller – and more recognizable as our modern racehorse. Indeed, he has changed little since the mid-nineteenth century, although strains vary according to speciality. For example, the sprinter, who races over short distances, tends to be tall and leggy, while the stayer is more compact and muscled. A combination of these two types makes the classic middle-distance horse.

"Today's racehorse is a horse of great beauty and presence, which he owes to his Arabian inheritance."

Left: *Pictured at Matahura in New Zealand, these retired racehorses enjoy an idyllic existence at the end of their careers on the track*

"The best Irish Drafts have strong, sound legs and straight, free action; they possess excellent shoulders and are natural jumpers."

LIKE THE Arabian, the Thoroughbred has, over the centuries, been used to refine and improve other stock. The Irish Draft, for example, is a light draft breed that made an excellent working farm horse; crossing with a Thoroughbred produces a superb sport horse that is unsurpassed.

Origins of the Irish Draft are largely unknown, although it is thought the ubiquitous Spanish horse features somewhere in the mix. French and Flemish horses imported into Ireland in the early twelfth century probably gave the indigenous Irish stock its size and character, and the breed was further refined using Spanish blood. The result is a big, strong horse – stallions can stand 17hh – with a comparatively small, intelligent head, which is perhaps due to the use of the Connemara pony in early stock.

The best Irish Drafts have strong, sound legs and straight, free action; they possess excellent shoulders and are natural jumpers. They are much in demand as show jumpers and hunters – across country, they are hard to beat. The Irish hunter is said to have an uncanny ability to "find an extra leg" – and thus get himself, and his rider, out of trouble – when jumping. The addition of Thoroughbred blood gives them added quality and speed.

Indeed, there are few "draft" type horses that are not improved with some Thoroughbred blood – show jumping aficionados will remember a good horse called Wiston Bridget, a Shire/Thoroughbred cross, who was ridden by Tim Stockdale with considerable success.

Left: *The origins of the Irish Draft are largely unknown, but adding Thoroughbred blood to the mix produces a superlative sport horse*

THE FRIESIAN breed owes much to the Andalucian of Spain (chapter 3). A cold blooded horse – as opposed to the "hot blooded" Thoroughbred or Arabian – he is a stocky draft horse based on the primitive Forest Horse of Europe. He was acknowledged by the Romans as being a superlative work horse. The breed takes its name from the Friesland region of The Netherlands and is thought to date back as far as 1000BC. Over the years, the breed did improve, as did its fortunes. The stocky horse, as well as being tough and hardy, had a sweet and biddable nature and made an excellent harness horse. He was also highly valued as a knight's charger. Although not a big horse, he had tremendous bearing and an impressive high-stepping action. During the Spanish occupation of The Netherlands in the Eighty Years War (1568-1648), the infusion of Spanish blood gave the breed more refinement.

In the nineteenth century, the Friesian – who was also widely worked as both a harness and saddle horse – was used extensively in the trotting races that were popular at the time and, as a consequence, faster and lighter specimens found favor. This was almost the end of the original Friesian, but, fortunately, a breeding plan was put into place to save the lines. Today's Friesian is a compact, beguiling little horse with spectacular paces and an endearing temperament. He stands at 15hh and has short, strong legs with hard feet and a well-muscled body. His long head has nobility and his expressive eye indicates his cheerful willingness. His neck is highly arched and he carries himself proudly. His extravagant, rippling mane and tail are reminiscent of those of the Andalucian and Lusitano. He is exclusively black, with no white markings, and Britain's Fell and Dales ponies (chapter 6) are thought to owe much to the Friesian, as does the UK's heavy breed, the Shire (chapter 8).

The Friesian has played a part in the development of other breeds, too, notably the Orlov Trotter of Russia; the Norfolk Trotter – a forebear of today's Hackney horse and pony – in England, and America's Morgan horse (chapter 5). Because of his black color and superb bearing, he is popular as a funeral horse, harnessed to the hearse and decked with black plumes. He has also found a niche in the circus and early Friesians were used in the riding schools of France and Spain, where they excelled at the movements of the *Haute École*. He is still in demand as a carriage horse, where his uniform black color makes him easy to match in a team – for competition or just for his enduring beauty.

Above and right: *The magnificent Friesian owes much to the Andalucian, whose influence can clearly be seen in his noble head and extravagant action*

"A compact little horse, the Friesian
has tremendous bearing and
impressive high-stepping action."

Left: Warmbloods combine elastic paces with an amenable temperament and traditional good looks

> "The warmblood is in great demand as a competition horse and virtually dominates the dressage arena."

Below: The Oldenburger is the heaviest of all the German Warmbloods, which include Hanoverian, Trakehner, and Holstein

AS A success story, there is little to beat the warmblood. In the twenty-first century, he is in great demand as a competition horse and virtually dominates the dressage stadium. The development of the warmblood began when breeders aimed to produce a horse that could be worked on the land, and used as a carriage horse or cavalry mount. As armaments became less heavy and cumbersome, a lighter, nimbler horse was required, and, eventually, there came the demand for a sleeker riding type, as equestrianism became less of a necessity and more of a recreational sport.

The modern warmblood is so-called because he derives from a mix of "hotblood" – such as Arabian or Thoroughbred – with "coldblood", the draft type based on the primitive Forest Horse. The result is a large, correct riding horse, combining elastic paces with good looks and an amenable temperament. Principal warmblood breeds include the Oldenburger – the heaviest of the German Warmbloods, as seen on these pages - Hanoverian, Trakehner, Holstein, Dutch, Danish and Swedish Warmbloods, and the Selle Français.

PERHAPS THE most successful of all warmbloods is the Hanoverian, who has excelled in both show jumping and dressage, and is in great demand as a competition horse. He is a handsome creature, with powerful limbs and a long, energetic stride.

The first Hanoverians were bred at Celle, a stud founded in 1735 by George II, Elector of Hanover and King of England. The foundation stallions were Holsteins, powerful coach horses, then Thoroughbred blood was introduced to refine the stock. The Thoroughbred influence can be seen in the Hanoverian head, which is clean cut with a large, intelligent eye. Hanoverians continue to be bred at Celle, where Thoroughbreds and Trakehners are still used to develop the stock further, and where the horses are routinely performance tested to ensure they live up to the Hanoverian ideal. Emphasis is placed on reliability, performance and temperament.

Previous pages: *The handsome Selle Français, or French Saddle Horse, is a versatile and popular warmblood*

Below, right and next pages: *The imposing Hanoverian is perhaps the most successful of all the warmblood breeds*

Above: *Originally a cavalry mount, the modern Holstein is in demand as a competition horse and hunter*

Left: *The use of oriental and Spanish blood, together with a strong Thoroughbred influence, has added quality to the Holstein*

THOROUGHBRED BLOOD has also played a part in refining the Holstein, who has, over the years, been developed from a cavalry mount to a scopey competition horse, much in demand as a hunter, show jumper, eventer and dressage horse. The modern Holstein, pictured on these pages, is much lighter than earlier examples of the breed, with a finer head and generally more quality.

There is evidence of Holstein types existing as far back as 1285 in the Schleswig-Holstein region from which he takes his name. Like many of the warmblood types, he benefited from the use of Spanish and oriental blood as well as Thoroughbred, which added quality to his superb temperament.

125

Above: *The Trakehner is perhaps the most elegant of all warmbloods*

Left: *Combining excellent conformation with athletic paces, the Trakehner is the ideal competition horse*

THE TRAKEHNER is perhaps the most elegant of all warmbloods and the closest to the competition horse ideal. Originating from East Prussia – now part of Lithuania – he was developed at the Royal Trakehner Stud founded by King Freidrich Wilhelm I in 1732 and was formerly known as the East Prussian Horse.

Again, use of Arabian and Thoroughbred blood has produced a lighter, finer stamp, and the influence of the latter can be seen in his handsome head, which some say has more character than that of other warmblood types. His long, elegant neck and well-shaped shoulders echo his Thoroughbred inheritance. He stands between 16-16.2hh and has excellent, well-balanced conformation, combined with athletic, free paces and stamina.

THE SIGHT of the "dancing white stallions" of the Spanish Riding School of Vienna is unforgettable – the magnificent horses leap and pirouette in the extraordinary "airs above the ground" with unimaginable athleticism and grace.

These are the world-famous Lipizzaners, derived largely from the Iberian horse (chapter 3) – acknowledged by the "Spanish" in the riding school's title – who take their name from where they were first bred in 1580, Lipizza (or Lipica), in what was then part of the Austro-Hungarian Empire.

A compact, muscular horse, the Lipizzaner is almost always grey, lightening to white, although bays are sometimes seen and one is always resident at the Vienna school. The school Lipizzaners are bred at Piber in Austria, but studs in Hungary, the Czech Republic and Romania also specialize in the breed. The modern Lipizzaner is based on just five stallions, who have their own distinct characteristics.

Above and left: *The world-famous Lipizzaner is a compact, muscular horse derived from the Iberian breeds*

SPANISH BLOOD appears, too, in the lineage of Britain's Cleveland Bay, a pack horse dating back to the Middle Ages. Formerly known as the Chapman Horse, he is one of Britain's oldest breeds.

Originally bred in the Cleveland Hills of Yorkshire, he worked the land and was used to transport huge loads of wool, on which much of the country's economy rested in the seventeenth century. He was then refined to meet demand for the taller, lighter carriage horse and is still used by England's royal courts today as a coach horse. He possesses excellent bone and substance, which he passes on when bred with other stock, and makes an outstanding riding horse.

He is also a good jumper, another characteristic which he is known to breed on and, when crossed with Thoroughbred blood, he makes a fine hunter. True to his name, the Cleveland Bay is always bay, with black points, and no white markings other than the occasional small white star.

Above and right: *In 2003, the Cleveland Bay was listed as "critical" by the Rare Breeds Survival Trust, which monitors numbers of Britain's indigenous equines. In a survey undertaken in 1997, there were just one hundred and fifty breeding females left in Britain*

Chapter 5

HORSES OF THE AMERICAS

HORSES OF THE AMERICAS

When horses were reintroduced to the New World in the sixteenth century, they terrified the early Native Americans, who had never before seen such a creature.

GIVEN THE enormous number and variety of equine breeds in North and South America, it is extraordinary to think that horses were not reintroduced to these continents until the sixteenth century. It is thought that equines existed in the Americas hundreds of thousands of years ago, crossing over the land bridge that then existed between the great continents. However, those early equines were hunted to extinction and there were no horses in the Americas for some eight thousand years, until the Spanish conquistadors ventured to the New World in the fifteenth century.

The Spaniards were to conquer Mexico and South America in the sixteenth century, with Hernán Cortés overcoming the Aztecs in his savage conquest of Mexico, and Francisco Pizzaro similarly crushing the Inca tribes of Peru. It is known that Cortés landed in Mexico in 1519, bringing with him – as well as his army – sixteen horses. Those early Spanish horses came as something of a shock to the Aztecs, who had never seen anything like them.

The horses wore armor, as did their riders, and appeared to the frightened native people as one creature combined,

man and beast, like a sort of centaur. When a rider fell to the ground, it appeared to the Aztecs that the terrifying creature was being ripped apart.

Of these original sixteen horses, eleven were stallions, two of which were skewbald or piebald or spotted, and five were mares. They were to form the basis of the USA's horse breeds, in which both spotted and broken-coated are legion.

Cortés's own horse, El Morzillo – The Black One – was injured during a foray to Honduras in 1524, when he damaged a foot so badly that he could go no further. Cortés left the horse in the care of some American Indians, with the intention to return for him, but he was never able to do so. Despite the best efforts of the superstitious Indians, who had no idea how to look after this strange animal, El Morzillo died, probably of malnutrition.

The Indians, fearing reprisals from the white man, created a statue of the horse, which came to be worshipped as the god Tziunchan – the God of Thunder and Lightning – until it was destroyed by missionary priests in 1697. By this time, however, the horse was firmly re-established in the New World.

The Mustang (chapter 1) almost certainly derived from those early horses – which were of Andalucian and Barb stock – some of which presumably escaped and started breeding in the wild. Similarly, the Galiceno pony of Mexico – which takes its name from Galicia in north-west Spain – is thought to derive from some of the earliest horses brought by the Spanish from the island of Hispaniola (now Haiti) in the sixteenth century. The first American breeding farm was founded on Hispaniola, with others following in Cuba, Puerto Rico and Jamaica.

Next to the Mustang, America's most famous breed is perhaps the Quarter Horse, whose name derives from the fact that he was bred to race over a quarter-mile (about four hundred meters). This name did not come, as is often mistakenly quoted, from the fact that he is a "quarter Thoroughbred".

The Quarter Horse was originally known as the American Quarter Running Horse, or Short Horse, as he raced over short distances, or, more grandly, as the Famous and Celebrated

Above: *The Quarter Horse's springy elastic paces make him a superb mount for almost any equestrian discipline*

Above left: *These Quarter Horse yearlings already show the curiosity that goes with the breed's unique intelligence*

Previous pages left: *Quarter Horses, America's most famous breed, have been produced to race short distances*

Previous pages right: *Stepping out proudly, a beautiful example of America's National Show Horse, a mix of Arabian and American Saddlebred blood*

Colonial Quarter Pather, and was first bred in Virginia and its environs on the east coast. He is descended from the early Spanish horses, with Arabian blood and then English stock. A cargo of seventeen English stallions and mares was first imported to Virginia in 1611. These horses were of the native running stock – which in England was to become the Thoroughbred (chapter 4) – and were probably closely related to the now extinct Galloway pony and the Irish Hobby, which was to become the Connemara.

America's oldest all-American breed, the Quarter Horse has twelve principal "families", all of which owe much to early Thoroughbred influences. The stallion Janus was imported in 1752 and, when he died in 1780, he left behind a son of the same name who founded the important Printer line. Sir Archy, a son of the Derby winner Diomed (chapter 4), was also influential in the development of the American Saddlebred. The Old Billy, Cold Deck, Shiloh and Steel Dust families trace back to Sir Archy, and Joe Bailey and Peter McCude, two of the most notable twentieth century sires, are his descendants.

Above: *Turned out in the lush pastures of Maryland, this Quarter Horse certainly looks capable of "turning on a dime"*

Above right: *This stunning pair show the typical compact and neat conformation of the breed, which is renowned for its agility*

Left: *The Quarter Horse can be any solid color, including grey, although the most common is chestnut*

The Quarter Horse was certainly bred for speed, though, and is still the fastest equine sprinter. He is comparatively small, standing little over 15hh. He has heavily muscled quarters and hindlegs – which give him his characteristic bursts of speed – and powerful forelegs.

The Quarter Horse may well have become defunct with the increase in popularity – due to the growing influence of the English Thoroughbred – of racing over great distances. However, his famed quarter-mile sprint was perhaps the least of his abilities.

The Quarter Horse is said to be able to "turn on a dime and toss you back nine cents change" and it is his agility that saved him for posterity. Although he originated on the Eastern Seaboard – or east coast – of North America, when people started to spread out across the vast continent in the nineteenth century, he was used as a harness horse as well as for riding.

In the western states, his speed, agility and intelligence made him a superb ranch horse, possessing an innate "cow sense". Perhaps this is not so surprising, given his Spanish origins – the Spanish horses were renowned for their prowess in the bull-ring.

His reputation as being a "sleepy little critter that can unwind like lightning" acknowledges his sweet, calm temperament as well as his versatility, and today the Quarter Horse Register is the world's largest studbook, with more than one and a half million of the breed recorded.

Combining agility and intelligence with an amiable nature, the compact little horse makes an ideal mount for almost everyone, from a novice child to an experienced cowhand.

Right: *This Leopard spot Appaloosa shows one of the five distinctive coat patterns of the breed – dark egg-shaped spots all over the body. Highly prized by the Indian tribes who bred him, the horse's markings were almost as important as his hardy and tractable nature*

"America's oldest all-American breed, the Quarter Horse has twelve principal "families", all of which owe much to early Thoroughbred influences."

Above *The Quarter Horse is one of the world's most popular breeds*

THE QUARTER Horse has become a valuable outcross in his own right, particularly with America's spotted horse, the Appaloosa. This striking and instantly recognisable breed was developed by the Nez Percé Indian tribe in the states of Oregon, Washington and Idaho, and takes its name from the Palouse river, one of the principal breeding regions.

It is known that the early Spanish imports contained spotted strains and those genes bred through. The Indians – who prized their distinctive markings as highly as their hardiness and willing temperaments – were strictly selective, gelding male horses deemed unsuitable for breeding and trading substandard mares with other tribes.

The modern Appaloosa has five recognisable coat patterns: Leopard, white with dark spots; Snowflake, white spots all over the body but concentrated over the hindquarters; Blanket, where the quarters may be white or spotted; Marble, a mottled pattern over the body, and Frost, white specks on a dark background.

As well as his striking coloring, the Appaloosa has other distinctive characteristics. His tail is usually sparse, which the Nez Percé deemed a practical feature, because it was less likely to become entangled in thorns and shrubs.

A white *sclera* encircling the eye is a breed requirement, as is mottled skin around the muzzle. His hard, sound feet are often vertically striped.

The Nez Percé Indians and their horses were almost wiped out by the US army in 1876, but the breed was revived and is one of the most popular.

Above: *This Appaloosa shows the white sclera around the eye and the mottling of the skin on the nose and lips that is a breed characteristic*

Right: *America's National Show Horse combines the beauty of the Arabian with the charisma of the Saddlebred*

"The American Saddlebred makes an excellent harness horse as well as a show-ring star."

Left and above: *American Saddlebred youngstock show the breed's beauty, much of it owed to the influence of the Thoroughbred, who is still king in Kentucky*

THE AMERICAN Saddlebred has been termed the "peacock of the show ring" and he combines his spectacular and unique paces with great presence. Originally called the Kentucky Saddler, the breed is based on two early pacers, the Canadian Pacer and the Narrangasett Pacer.

A practical animal as well as a striking one, the Saddlebred is reminiscent of the English Hackney, with his flashy, high-stepping gait, and makes an excellent harness horse as well as a show-ring star. Bred principally in Kentucky's Blue Grass country, the horse has benefited from Thoroughbred blood.

The Saddlebred is sometimes called "America's most misunderstood breed" and his "bad press" is undoubtedly due in some part to his artificial show-ring image of a nicked, high-set tail and overlong feet. But he is a most handsome horse with striking paces, which in the "five-gaited" Saddlebred include a four-beat prancing movement and a full-speed high-stepping "rack".

Above *A Thoroughbred mare shows off her racehorse paces*

Left: *This thoroughbred foal enjoys his early days at one of the USA's major Thoroughbred studs. The American Thoroughbred world revolves around its "capital", Lexington, Kentucky. Here stands a statue of Man O' War, also known as Big Red, one of the most famous Thoroughbreds of the twentieth century. He was only beaten once and when he died in 1947, more than a thousand people attended his funeral*

Right: *The popularity of the Thoroughbred has increased throughout the world*

Above, right and above right: *The Rocky Mountain Pony has an unusual rich chocolate coat that does not appear in other descendants of the early Spanish imports. The full, flaxen mane and tail is a breed trait of the Rocky Mountain Pony and he is a generally good-looking, compact animal*

I F THE Saddlebred is renowned for his beauty, the Rocky
Mountain Pony was bred purely for his practicality. Like
most US horses, his origins are with the Spanish imports, but
the breed owes its development to one Sam Tuttle, from
Kentucky, and a foundation stallion called Old Tobe. Tuttle
provided horses for all levels of riders and Old Tobe passed his
smooth paces, pleasing conformation and amenable
temperament to his progeny.

Although no breed standard has been set for the Rocky
Mountain – there are only some two hundred recorded since
the register was first opened in 1986 – he is a compact
animal, standing between 14.2–14.3hh. And while he was
developed as a practical, rather than ornamental, breed, he is
undeniably good looking, possessing a coloring which is
unusual in other equine breeds.

THE PERUVIAN Paso, and the related Paso Fino, is equally, if not more, good-looking, and bears striking similarities to his Andalucian cousins. Like the Saddlebred and the Tennessee Walking Horse, these horses have distinctive gaits. The word *"paso"* means step. The Peruvian Paso was first established in Peru, South America, from horses brought over by the Spanish adventurer Francisco Pizarro. The horse is thought to be one-quarter Andalucian and three-quarters Barb. The Paso Fino is a related breed from Puerto Rico.

Right and below: *The Paso Fino of Puerto Rico (right) is strongly linked with the Peruvian Paso (below), which originated from Spanish horses brought over to the New World by Francisco Pizarro*

Above: *The Peruvian Paso has an arched, muscular neck and fine, abundant mane and tail. Bay and chestnut are most common, but all solid colors are seen and broken-coated is also acceptable*

Left: *This Paso Fino stallion shows the fire and spirit, as well as the beauty, of the breed and also illustrates the similarity between the Paso and the Andalucian, to which he is closely related*

Next pages: *The Peruvian Paso has very distinctive gaits, including the* paso fino, paso corto *and* paso largo, *which he inherits rather than learns*

Developed by highly selective breeding over a period of three hundred years, the Paso's most distinctive feature is his lateral gait, for which he is famed. His forelegs display extravagant, dishing action, while his powerful hindlegs and lowered quarters drive him forward.

There are three gaits – the *paso fino*, a collected, elevated movement; the *paso corto*, an easy traveling pace, and the *paso largo*, an extended fast gait which the horse can sustain for some distance and which is extremely comfortable for his rider. He is not a big horse, usually standing between 14-15hh, but is hardy and possesses great stamina, being able to maintain a steady speed of eleven miles (seventeen and a half kilometers) per hour over the rough and difficult terrain which is often encountered in his homeland.

The Paso Fino of Puerto Rico has the same gaits, which are his natural paces – inherited rather than taught. Distinctive gaits are seen in two other American breeds, including the Saddlebred and the Tennessee Walking Horse.

THE TENNESSEE Walking Horse is named for his gliding, running walk, at which he can maintain speeds of up to nine miles (fourteen and a half kilometers) per hour. Descended from Spanish stock, he also possesses Thoroughbred, Morgan and Saddlebred blood and exhibits three exceptional gaits: the flat walk, the running walk and a smooth comfortable canter. All these actions, as in the Paso, are inherited rather than taught. It is said of the breed that if you "ride one today you will buy one tomorrow", due to his supremely comfortable gait. He was particularly favored by the plantation owners of the Deep South as a conveyance from which to inspect their crops.

A large-boned, short-coupled, plain horse, he has a reliable, steady temperament and is an ideal choice as a family horse or a mount for novice or nervous riders. All colors are seen but black and chestnut are most popular.

Left and above: *The Tennessee Walking Horse is another of America's unique gaited breeds*

NOWHERE ELSE in the world is the Paint – formerly known as the Pinto – designated a breed, rather than a color. He has breed status only in America and that only comparatively recently, being recognized as a breed in 1963. He got his original name from the Spanish word for painted, pintado, and it is a good description.

He is further defined as Overo or Tobiano. Overo describes a dark coat with splashes of white and is most commonly found in South America, while Tobiano is white with large well-defined dark patches, and is found in North America. He generally stands between 15–16hh.

Below: *This handsome American Paint is what is called an Overo, chestnut with white patches. The Paint, or Pinto, takes his name from the Spanish* pintado, *or painted*

Above: *The Paint horse was a favorite mount of American Indians, as his broken coat was thought to be good camouflage, as these young horses illustrate*

"Nowhere else in the world is the Paint – formerly known as the Pinto – designated a breed, rather than a color"

Left: *The Overo, a dark coat with splashes of white, is thought to be due to a recessive gene, while the Tobiano, white with large dark patches, is dominant*

Above: *The Paint, or Pinto, horse only has breed status in the USA, and the Paint Horse Association divides horses into four types – stock, hunter, pleasure and saddle*

Right: *The Missouri Fox Trotter, one of the least known American breeds, was originally bred for racing, but his smooth comfortable action and ability to travel great distances at speed soon made him a popular choice for riding*

Left: *The cream or golden-colored Palamino, another horse familiar to viewers of Western movies, and registered as a breed in the USA*

Left: *It is thought that the sire of the original Morgan was either a Thoroughbred, a Friesian or a Welsh Cob. The authority Anthony Dent maintains that "there can be little doubt that Justin Morgan was a Welsh Cob with a touch of either Thoroughbred or Arabian"*

Below: *This handsome Morgan stallion shows the breed's fine, straight head and kind, intelligent outlook*

OF ALL the American breeds, the Morgan Horse is the oldest, and is unique in that it can be traced back to one single horse – originally called Figure, but named after his owner, Justin Morgan, on the latter's death. He was foaled in about 1790 and was acquired by his eponymous owner as a two-year-old. Although he only stood about 14hh, he was tremendously strong as well as extremely prepotent, passing on his strength, endurance and his high-stepping gait to his offspring.

His breeding is not known, although theories abound that his sire was a Thoroughbred, a Friesian or a Welsh Cob. Whatever the Morgan's original roots, he is a tough little horse with a charming nature and has been an important influence on the later American breeds.

Chapter 6

PONIES OF THE WORLD

PONIES OF THE WORLD

Intelligent, crafty, cunning, and kind by turn, the pony
can turn on the charm to capture the hardest heart.

ANGELIC AND cheeky in equal measure, the pony, with his charm and charisma, wins the hearts of the tiniest child and the most hardened adult. Intelligent, crafty, cunning but ultimately kind, he knows exactly how to get his own way – and we invariably let him.

The world is a melting pot of pony breeds, and both the Arabian (chapter 2) and the Iberian horse (chapter 3) appear in their lineage. Great Britain, however, has some of the oldest and most prized ponies – her nine native breeds are revered worldwide and the bloodlines exported all over the world.

The Exmoor pony, for example, native to the moor of the same name on the border of North Devon and West Somerset, appears in the Domesday Book in 1085, but is thought to trace back to the Celtic ponies of the Pleistocene Age. But Spanish blood crops up in his lineage too; in 1815 a stallion, known as Katerfelto, ran on the moor. Although he was captured, it has never been determined whence he came. He was a buckskin horse with black points and a distinctive eel stripe. Buckskin ponies are occasionally seen on Exmoor today and, with bay and brown, are the only permitted colors.

Previous page: *The Exmoor pony possesses great charm and, despite his diminutive size, can carry a light adult rider.*

Above: *The Exmoor has distinctive mealy markings around his muzzle and "toad eyes", heavily hooded as protection against*

Above right and right: *Tough and hardy, the Exmoor lives a semi-feral existence on the moor of the same name.*

Possessing great charm, the Exmoor today is a stocky, hardy little chap, with a pretty head and distinctive mealy markings on his muzzle. He also has so-called "toad eyes", heavily hooded as protection again the elements. Living a semi-feral existence, although some of the herds are owned, the ponies do tend to be skittish around humans and can be nervous of dogs, perhaps recalling an atavistic threat from wolf packs.

Another peculiarity to the breed is an "ice tail", a thick fan-like growth of hair at the top of the tail which gives protection against rain, sleet, and snow. The breed also exhibits the beginnings of a seventh molar, which is not found in any other equine breed.

The Exmoor, for all his strength and toughness, makes a good child's pony as he is generally sweet-natured. Sadly, though, the Exmoor pony is currently on the Rare Breeds Survival Trust register, listed as "endangered".

> *"For all his strength and toughness, the Exmoor makes a good child's pony as he is generally sweet-natured."*

Below: *The Dartmoor's long, low action and conformation make him a superb child's pony and, crossed with Thoroughbred or Arabian blood, he makes an excellent all-rounder*

THE EXMOOR pony's neighbor, the Dartmoor, of mid and south Devon, is also an endangered breed. This little pony was almost wiped out completely during World War Two.

The breed's origins are thought to lie with the Old Devon Pack Horse and the delightfully named Cornish Goonhilly pony, although both these breeds are now extinct. Over time, the Dartmoor has been improved with both Welsh and Arabian blood, but an outcross with Shetlands to produce pit ponies was disastrous for the breed.

It would be tragic if the Dartmoor were allowed to die out, for with his comfortable action and biddable nature he makes a superb riding pony and, when crossed with Thoroughbred or Arabian blood, an excellent all-rounder. He has hard, sound feet and a distinctive long, low action, which makes him a wonderful child's pony. Bay, brown or black pure Dartmoors have little or no white markings.

"The breed's origins are thought to lie with the Old Devon Pack Horse and the delightfully named Cornish Goonhilly pony."

Above: *Like the Exmoor pony, the Dartmoor is registered with the Rare Breeds Survival Trust as "endangered"*

Left: *Dartmoor ponies can be bay, brown or black – this little skewbald is not pure Dartmoor and would not be acceptable in the breed society*

IF IT is a child's first pony you are looking for, you could do little better than a New Forest. Intelligent, sweet-tempered and willing, they are surefooted and docile.

The breed has had a great deal of outside influence; as early as the thirteenth century, ponies are recorded in the Forest, which lies in Hampshire, and it is known that the Thoroughbred Marske – sire of the great Eclipse – served some of the Forest mares in the eighteenth century. Arabian and Barb blood was added to the mix in the nineteenth century. In 1918-19 the polo pony Field Marshall stood in the Forest, adding greatly to the development of the breed. Many leading dressage ponies carry New Forest blood.

A robust, adaptable animal, his long, low action and sweeping canter make him in demand as a riding pony. The upper height limit is 14.2hh, which means the New Forest can easily carry adults.

Top: *Seen here in his hardy winter coat, living a semi-wild existence in the New Forest, the modern New Forest pony is a robust, adaptable animal, who has benefited from outside influence in his breeding*

Above: *The New Forest has a long, low stride and sweeping canter and can carry both adults and children*

THE CONNEMARA is another native that makes an exceptionally good riding pony, for adults and children. The breed takes its name from the wild country on the western coast of Ireland and is the country's only indigenous pony. Its forerunner, the Irish Hobby, together with the Galloway pony, played a major part in the development of the Thoroughbred, and the Connemara later benefited from Arabian and, surprisingly, Clydesdale blood. The influence of Oriental outcrosses can be seen in the modern Connemara's pretty head. Welsh and Thoroughbred blood further improved the stock, which has earned the reputation of being one of the best pony breeds in the world.

While the most common color was buckskin with black points and a dark dorsal stripe, most Connemaras today are grey, although bay and brown are accepted. With their origins in the wild, boggy marshland of Ireland, they are exceptionally hardy ponies with well-made legs and sound feet, which make them good jumpers.

Top and above: *Most Connemara ponies are grey, but bay and brown are also seen*

173

BOTH THE Dales and Fell ponies of northern England are also listed by the Rare Breeds Survival Trust, the former as "vulnerable", and the latter as "endangered". The Fell, recognized since Roman times, was used for draft work and transportation. Cistercian monks also used them and it is thought that they introduced the color grey, as "white" stock was the sign of monastic ownership. Other more commonly seen colors are black, brown, or bay. Strong and hardy, although standing under 14hh, Fells are now used for riding, driving, and farm work. They are also useful for logging, their agility and surefootedness making them able to move on the forested slopes too steep for tractors.

The Dales pony was in great demand as a farm horse and for his ability to carry heavy loads of lead from the mines across rough terrain to the north-east ports. He was also used by the army as a mountain artillery pack pony.

Standing a little taller than the Fell, he has exceptionally good paces, which make him an ideal riding and driving pony. Welsh Cob and Clydesdale blood has been used in the breed, the latter's influence occasionally cropping up in a grey Dales, although the predominant color is black. The Welsh Cob blood – introduced about a hundred years ago in the form of a stallion called Comet – ensures the Dales retains his wonderful action.

His earlier origins, however, probably lie with the Friesian, to whom he still bears a resemblance. He has a handsome head, set on to a fairly short, thick-set neck, and a strong, muscular body. His luxurious mane and tail is balanced with generous feather on the lower leg. His kind and tractable nature make him an ideal child's mount, while his strength means he can carry an adult with ease.

Above: *The Dales pony, like the Fell, is known for his strength and he has exceptionally good paces*

Above right: *Fell ponies are strong and hardy, and can be used for riding, driving, and farm work – the breed has been recognized since Roman times*

Right: *The Highland is thought to trace back to the ancient Forest pony*

SCOTLAND'S HIGHLAND pony is another thought to trace back to the ancient Forest pony, which formed the basis for the Friesian. There were two types of Highland, the smaller pony from the Western Isles and the larger, heavier one from the mainland. Today, they have integrated and the two distinct types have been lost, apart from a semi-feral herd on the remote island of Rhum, which are the smaller type and retain the old variations of the breed's buckskin coloring, which can vary from cream to grey, mouse or fox. Most solid colors are now seen – including a striking liver chestnut – usually with a dorsal stripe and zebra markings on the legs. His neat, pretty head shows the influence of the Arabian, with small ears and large, kind eyes. He has a long, crested neck, with a short, strong back and muscular quarters.

Moulded by the harsh Scottish climate, the Highland has evolved into a tough and hardy pony who can undertake almost any task. The Scottish crofters used him for riding, driving, packing, and working the land and his toughness and calm demeanor mean he is still in demand among deer stalkers in the Highlands. The Highland's generous nature makes him an excellent all-rounder – and crossing with a Thoroughbred produces a superlative hunter.

"The Highland's neat, pretty head shows the influence of the Arabian, with small ears and large, kind eyes."

Right: *A Highland mare and her foal*

THERE CAN be few harsher places than the Shetland Isles off the Scottish coast. The hardiness of the Isles' indigenous breed is legendary, as is its strength – pound for pound the Shetland pony is believed to be the strongest known equine. The Shetland is an ancient breed, believed to have strong links to ponies from Scandinavia, which may have reached the Scottish isles before the lands were separated by water in around 8000BC. Although these ponies would have been influenced by the Celtic pony, taken to Scotland in the second and third centuries AD, the appearance of the Shetland has probably changed little in subsequent centuries.

He has a small, well-shaped head, with neat ears and wide forehead, a sign of the breed's inherent intelligence. His large nostrils allow the air to warm before it reaches his lungs, a trait often found in equines from northern latitudes, and a supremely waterproof double coat in winter helps repel the rain and wind.

The Shetland Pony Studbook Society, which sets the breed standard for registered ponies, is split into "miniature" ponies, standing up to thirty-four inches at the shoulder, and "standard", between thirty-four and forty-two inches, which is the upper height limit. Any color is permitted, including skewbald and piebald, except spotted.

Left and right: *Shetland ponies can be any solid color, piebald or, like this one, skewbald, but spotted is not permitted by the Studbook*

"He should have the dished face of the Arabian, the muscled body of the Quarter Horse and the distinctive patterning of the Appaloosa."

INCREASINGLY POPULAR in Europe, the Shetland has also found a large fan base in the USA, to the extent that an "American Shetland" has been developed. Crossed with Hackney ponies and later small Arabian horses, he is flashier than the original breed. He was also used to develop the Pony of the Americas; a Shetland stallion was crossed with an Appaloosa to create a strikingly spotted coat.

The man credited with the development of the Pony of the Americas was a lawyer called Les Boomhower of Mason City, Iowa. He was offered an Arabian-Appaloosa mare and her colt, whom he was to name Black Hand, who was white with black patches over his body.

Les named the foal thus because of a pattern of black spots on the colt's flank that formed a hand. It was these unusual markings that gave the lawyer the idea to form the Pony of the Americas Club. He bred the colt to Shetland mares and the resulting POA – as the breed became known – had to conform to strict guidelines.

The pony could be no less than forty-four inches and no more than fifty-two inches. He should have the dished face of the Arabian, the muscled body of the Quarter Horse and the distinctive patterning of the Appaloosa, visible at a distance of forty feet.

The breed, intended for children, although he could be used as a driving pony for adults, grew and grew – in all senses of the word. From Black Hand, registered to the club in 1954, by 1996 the registry recorded 40,000 and the height standard was increased to between forty-six and fifty-four inches in 1963, the upper limit being raised to fifty-six inches in 1985.

With Welsh, Mustang and Indian ponies being added to the mix, the Pony of the Americas became more of a little horse, but retained his wide-ranging appeal.

Left: *The Pony of the Americas was founded by crossing a Shetland stallion with an Appaloosa mare*

Left: *The increasingly popular miniature Shetland stands no higher than thirty-four inches at the shoulder*

Right: *These miniature Shetland foals already display the neat pretty head of the breed and are full of intelligence*

Below right: *Shetland ponies are remarkably hardy and thrive in the harsh conditions of their native land*

Below: *Shetlands, particularly miniatures, have a strong fan base in the USA, so much so that the US now has a distinct Shetland strain*

"The hardiness of the Isles' indigenous breed is legendary, as is its strength – pound for pound the Shetland pony is believed to be the strongest known equine."

WORLDWIDE, PERHAPS the most popular pony breed is the Welsh Mountain (Section A), a beguiling little creature with the Arabian's dished face and wide eye. He stands no taller than 12hh and makes a splendid child's pony.

But do not dismiss him as a "pretty toy"; the Welsh pony, which provides the foundation of all four sections of the Welsh Pony and Cob Society Studbook, is a tough character, for whom the "survival of the fittest" adage rings true. He is tough and hardy, able to survive on the meagre rations his forefathers found on the Welsh mountains, and is courageous, spirited and kind.

It is known that the Romans were the first to improve the indigenous Welsh stock by adding eastern blood. Thoroughbred blood was also introduced in the form of Merlin, a direct descendant of The Darley Arabian, and the modern Welsh pony owes much to a stallion called Dyoll Starlight, whose dam was said to be a "miniature Arabian".

The Section B is similar to the Welsh Mountain but is more of a riding pony. Standing up to 13.2hh, he has a long and low action, as opposed to the higher knee action of the Welsh Mountain, but retains the inherent soundness and good, hard feet.

The Welsh Cobs, too, make excellent riding ponies and, as they are bigger than the pony sections, are suitable for adults as well as children. The main difference between the two sections is size; the section C, Welsh pony of Cob type, stands up to 13.2hh, while the section D Welsh Cob has no upper height limit. Described as "the best ride and drive animal in the world", the Welsh Cob derived from crossing the Welsh Mountain with Roman imports. Further improvements were made in the eleventh and twelfth centuries by using Spanish and possibly Barb horses. The new blood resulted in the development of the Welsh Cart Horse, now extinct, and the Powys Cob. The latter, crossed with Norfolk Roadsters and Yorkshire Coach Horses in the eighteenth and nineteenth centuries, became the modern Welsh Cob.

He is a bigger version of the Welsh Mountain – in silhouette he should look just like the Section A – with a quality pony head and good bone. Spirited, courageous and strong, his stamina makes him an excellent hunter and outcrossing with Thoroughbred blood produces a superb competition horse. He is renowned for his spectacular, flashy trot, which is why he is so popular as a harness horse, but his speed and scope mean he is just as in demand as a riding horse.

Above and above left: *Welsh Cobs have quality pony heads and good bone, with a spectacular trot – crossed with Thoroughbred blood, they make excellent competition horses*

Following pages: *The Welsh Cob – section D of the studbook – is renowned as the "best ride and drive pony in the world"*

IT IS said of Austria's charming Haflinger pony that once seen, he is never forgotten and, indeed, this striking pony has increased in popularity, particularly in the driving world.

The breed originated in the South Tyrol, where the native Tyrolean pony was crossed with Arabians brought back from the continental wars. The resulting hardy mountain breed – which takes its name from the village of Hafling, in what is now northern Italy – was worked on the Alpine farms.

Although standing little over 14hh, the Haflinger is strong for his size, and his beauty – he is always bright chestnut with flaxen mane and tail – means he is now bred in more than twenty countries.

"The Haflinger is always chestnut – ranging in shades from gold to rust – with flaxen mane and tail."

Below and right: *Haflingers are strong ponies, despite their diminutive size*

Left and right: *To the Icelandic people, their native breed is a miniature horse, not a pony, and the breed has been kept pure*

Below: *The Icelandic Horse has five gaits, including the* tolt, *which is a very fast running walk that can cross broken ground*

TO THE people of Iceland, their native breed is never a pony, despite the fact that he stands little over 13hh; he is always the Icelandic Horse. It is thought that horses were first brought to Iceland in the first century by the Norsemen, who settled on this volcanic island.

The Icelandic stock is extremely pure, largely because the country's government banned outside bloodlines as long ago as 930AD, after a disastrous experiment with eastern blood to improve the breed. He is a stocky, plain little horse, with a heavy head and short body. Known as a five-gaited horse, the Icelandic performs the distinctive *tolt*, a fast running walk that can cross broken ground at speed. The breed society describes it as a "gait which with unaltered footfall can escalate its swiftness from a mere stop to great speed".

Above: *Norway's Fjord pony bears a strong resemblance to the historic Przewalski in his buckskin coloring and dorsal markings*

NORWAY'S FJORD pony, who used to be worked by loggers, has perhaps had some influence on the Icelandic Horse, a similar type, as Viking warriors took him on raids throughout Scandinavia. He bears a strong resemblance to ancient wild Przewalski's Horse (chapter 1) in his buckskin coloring with dorsal stripe and zebra markings, and his coarse erect mane.

Right and above right: *The Caspian oozes quality from head to tail*

LIKE THE Icelandic breed, the Caspian – although standing between 10-12hh – is more of a small horse than a pony. This ancient breed – a native of the area around the Elburtz Mountains and Caspian Sea in what was Persia – was thought to have become extinct until a few were found pulling carts in northern Iran in 1965.

195

"The Caspian is thought to be a "prototype" of the Arabian and has many similar characteristics in miniature, but he predates the Arabian by about three thousand years."

He is thought to have been a distant "prototype" of the Arabian and has many Arabian characteristics in miniature, including the concave profile and short, neat ears. He has the fine hair on his face and large, liquid eyes, but the breed pre-dates the Arabian by about three thousand years. He is of narrow build, with strong sloping shoulders; he has a short back and carries his full tail very high, like the Arabian. Usual colors are bay, grey and brown, while black and cream

are sometimes also seen. The Caspian has good, dense bone and very strong, oval feet. The little horse oozes quality from head to tail.

Although spirited, he is willing and tractable, with exceptional jumping ability, which makes him a superb child's ride. The Caspian has a long and floating action and can keep up with the average horse at all paces except the full gallop. He is also strong, so performs well in harness.

Chapter 7
FOALS

FOALS

Most would agree that all baby animals are, at the very least, cute, but there is something about the foal's long-legged gawkiness that has a charm all of its own.

INQUISITIVE AND fearless, the young foal is into everything; from the moment he is born, it appears to be his intention to explore everything, watched anxiously by his devoted mother. The whole world is there for the taking.

Born in the wild, it is imperative that foals stand immediately, albeit shakily, on their impossibly spindly legs, because the herd has no idea where the next threat, the next predator, is lying in wait. A young foal would make an easy meal. Despite their domestication, horses still have this inherent urgency and the first thing a new mother will do is nudge her reluctant offspring to his feet.

But, merely moments old – a newborn will usually be standing within one hour – he will be up, wobbling perilously, while his anxious mother licks him from head to feet, cleaning him and stimulating his blood supply. Once up, the next most

important action for the newborn is to feed; his first taste of his mother's milk – called the colostrum – is vital, because it contains essential antibodies that the baby needs to survive and which will be quickly absorbed by his gut. He should take at least one and a half pints of colostrum within six hours of birth. It is rare for horses and ponies to give birth to more than a single foal, although it does happen. Horse breeders generally try to avoid this as it usually means two weak babies instead of one strong one. In the wild, twins rarely survive.

Mares come into season – also called coming "on heat" – every eighteen to twenty-one days and the ideal time for foals to be born, whether wild or domesticated, is the early spring, so they can make the most of the lusher grazing when they are weaned, or no longer taking their mother's milk. The dam needs sustenance too, so she will also benefit.

Previous pages left: *A Quarter Horse foal confidently follows his palomino mother*

Previous pages right: *This delightful Welsh foal shows all the charm and beauty of the breed*

Above: *Mares with young foals are fiercely protective of their babies*

Above right: *In Britain, the "birthday" of every Thoroughbred, no matter what date he was actually born, is 1 January*

Right: *This Exmoor foal already has the mealy muzzle typical of the breed*

The mare carries her foal for eleven months and the resulting offspring will be reliant on his mother's milk for up to six months. It is a steep learning curve for the newborn. A wild foal should be standing within an hour of birth, and shortly after he should be able to walk and feed. Soon afterward, he should be able to canter and to call out to his mother. Horses and ponies are creatures of flight and nature intends the foal to flee from danger at his mother's side.

During the first hour of his existence, a process called imprinting will take place, ensuring an unbreakable and irreversible bond with his mother and with her to him. It is vital that this process is not disturbed. The bond is incredibly strong, so much so that if the mare and her foal are separated accidentally, they will ignore all obstacles and injuries in their efforts to be reunited.

The foal relies on his mother entirely for the first few weeks of life, becoming braver and more independent as he grows stronger. In a herd environment, he will soon be made aware of the pecking order and will learn where he is welcome and where he is not. In growing up with a mixed groups of horses or ponies of all ages, including the herd stallion, the youngster gets the chance to learn all aspects of horse behavior and, more importantly, discipline. He will usually be tolerated, provided he knows his place, and discipline meted out by older horses is both harsh and fair.

Above: *A striking Trakehner foal, with a large white star and bright bay coloring*

Above right: *A chestnut mare and chestnut stallion will always produce a chestnut foal, like this Arabian*

> "Foals born in breeds of exclusively grey horses are always born brown or black and their coat changes color as they grow."

Left: *The distinctive coloring of this foal is common in Highland ponies, which can vary from the light "fox" to darker "mouse" buckskin*

Foals are born all colors – the pretty buckskin foal (far left) displays one of the most common colors of Highland ponies, although all shades of buckskin, from light "fox" to the darker "mouse". The little chestnut Arabian (above) clearly takes after his mother, while the Trakehner foal (left) appears to be a bright bay to his dam's more sombre brown.

But colors at birth can be very deceptive. Foals born in breeds of exclusively grey horses – like the Camargue (chapter 1) or the famous Lipizzaners of the Spanish Riding School (chapter 4) – are always born brown or black and their coat changes color as they grow. This is why foals in sales catalogues, particularly those of Thoroughbreds, may be described as bay/brown/grey.

For the purpose of simple genetics, grey is known to be a dominant color, followed by bay, brown, black and chestnut. Chestnut is recessive, so a chestnut stallion mated to a chestnut mare will always produce a chestnut foal – our little Arabian will retain his color. However, it is entirely possible for a bay stallion and a bay mare to produce a chestnut foal.

Above left: This foal is clearly going to

Above: What delightful markings this miniature horse has. Broken-

"*Such is the demand for lovely things in small packages, the Shetland Pony Studbook is now divided into standard and miniature.*"

Above left: *This little chestnut miniature has a real "look at me" quality*

Above right: *Miniatures are popular in the US; they come in all variations of equine colors and are referred to as miniature horses, rather than ponies*

The little chestnut charmer (above left) again has his mother's color, although his mealy muzzle gives him his own unique character. The youngsters (above) show a great variety of colors and at least one of them appears to have inherited his dam's broken coat. These ponies are miniatures, bred in America, although aficionados prefer to refer to them as miniature "horses". Incidentally, the term "pony" is a relatively new one; it is thought to derive from the seventeenth century French *poulenet* – which means "foal".

Perhaps the best-known miniature horse is the American Falabella, which is now exceedingly rare – there are thought to be less than eight hundred Falabellas registered to the breed society. These little horses originate from Argentina.

The UK's most famous "miniature" is, of course, the Shetland pony and such is the demand for "lovely things in small packages", the Shetland Pony Studbook is now divided into standard and miniature, the latter standing less than thirty-four inches at the shoulder.

It should be remembered, however, that these beguiling little creatures are still equines and not merely pets – indeed, they can be stubborn and wilful, so need to be shown who is boss if they are not to behave in an unsociable manner!

Above: *An exuberant Arabian foal shows his free, elastic paces*

Above left: *As he grows in confidence, the foal will gradually play further away from his dam, although at the slightest hint of danger he will quickly return to her side*

> "*As the foal matures, he will become less dependent on his mother.*"

Left: *This warmblood mare and her upstanding foal stride out confidently*

As the foal matures, he will become less dependent on his mother – there's a huge world out there, and he will want to explore every inch of it. If he is born into a herd environment, he will soon interact with other foals. Playful and boisterous, the youngsters will romp and gallop about and stage mock fights, with much squealing and kicking, which can look quite ferocious. Although they are playing, the babies are actually beginning to assert themselves and to find their place in the herd. They are also testing their survival techniques.

While the adult horses are capable of inflicting considerable damage on a foal, generally a youngster's irritating inquisitive nature is tolerated by his elders, even the senior stallions. Usually, a flattening of ears and head-tossing by a member of the older generation is enough warning to a baby that he is seriously getting on their nerves. When approaching a member of the herd, a foal may adopt what appears to be an exaggerated nursing position – neck and muzzle extended, with his ears flattened out to the sides – and repeatedly snapping his jaws together. This is submissive behavior designed to placate the older horse, but when frightened youngsters may well display it later in life.

Early days are an idyllic existence that is spent feeding, playing and sleeping. At eight to ten days, he will be starting to nibble grass, although not in great quantities for the first few weeks. While he sleeps, his mother will "stand guard" over him, watchful for any threat – real or imagined – to her young.

"Early days are an idyllic existence that is spent feeding, playing and sleeping."

Right: *A Trakehner foal stops for a rest*

Above: *A Connemara foal enjoys the warm days of spring*

Above left: *Already displaying the high-stepping action for which the breed is renowned, this Welsh Cob foal is full of life*

Left: *A beautifully marked Paint foal*

Growing older and stronger, the foal will sleep less and play more, and at an increasing distance from his mother. Play develops his co-ordination and balance and reinforces survival techniques – but, when frightened or alarmed, he will instinctively return to his mother's side and will often suckle simply for comfort.

If the foal's dam becomes pregnant again, she will gradually wean her existing youngster by becoming increasingly more aggressive toward him as her pregnancy progresses.

Above: *This handsome fellow is a Lusitano, one of the noble Iberian breeds. He is already losing his baby characteristics and showing signs of the beauty he will have at maturity*

As they grow, like children, horses and ponies develop areas of their anatomy ahead of others – the little Chincoteague (above right) has a comparatively large head and neck. The adorably woolly Clydesdale foal (right) appears to have hardly any neck at all, while the thicker hair and feather on his sturdy legs are a breed characteristic.

In the wild, if a foal's dam is not in-foal again, he may continue to suckle until puberty, which occurs at around nine to twelve months old. In domesticated horses, it used to be considered the right time to wean a foal at five to six months.

Above: *This little Chincoteague's head looks too big for his gangly legs and short-coupled body*

Above right: *This Clydesdale already has some fine feathering on his lower limbs*

"As he grows older and stronger, the foal will sleep less and play more, and at an increasing distance from his mother."

Right: *As he matures, this fine foal gains the confidence to venture a little further from his mother's side*

Above: *These warmblood foals show no discomfort at being apart from their dams*

Above right: *Interaction with his peers is a vital part of the foal's development*

Above far right: *If the mare is not in-foal again, her foal may suckle for up to twelve months in the wild*

Previous pages: *Turned out with other youngsters, foals will soon form friendships*

There is a growing opinion that weaning a foal too early – unless there is a good reason to do so, such as his mother having little milk – can leave him psychologically scarred. Gradual methods of weaning are now much more widely used and many breeders agree that there is no need to wean foals as early as six months. Most healthy broodmares can support a nursing foal until shortly before giving birth again.

It was once advocated that separating mother and baby completely – out of sight and earshot – was the best way to wean the foal, the theory being that both parties soon "get over it". But most breeders would now agree that this process is highly unnatural and distressing and could have far-reaching consequences in later life. It could also have more immediate

repercussions, as the foal could inflict injuries on himself as he desperately tries to escape to get back to his mother.

A far more humane method is adopted in many studs, where a number of mares with foals of similar ages are turned out together to allow friendships to develop among the youngsters. Then one mare is led away from the group when they are turned out into the paddock and her foal quickly gets over his distress in the company of his peers and other mares. A couple of days later the process is repeated with another mare and so on until all the mares have been separated from their young. At a year old, theoretically at least, horses are capable of breeding, and so fillies and colts are usually split up at this stage.

Although the foal's "imprinting" with his mother should not be interrupted, humans can use this same instinct to encourage the foal to become accustomed to being handled. If a youngster learns that having his belly stroked, his ears caressed and legs rubbed are pleasurable experiences, it will make later treatment of him that much easier.

Stroking his legs, for instance, will help him to accept the farrier when the time comes, and if the foal accepts being rubbed all over, the vet will have no trouble when he needs to give the youngster an injection. If he grows accustomed to his mouth being touched, it will be easier for him to accept the bit when he is being broken to ride. All this attention should be given in small doses, as foals tire easily.

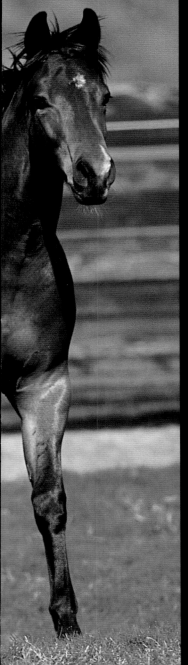

Above left and right *Like young humans, at puberty horses need stimulating, entertaining, educating and disciplining. For domesticated equines, their education should already have started, almost from the beginning*

Right: *This young Appaloosa has beautiful liver-spot markings*

Left: *Quarter Horse yearlings are both curious and confident*

It is an endorsement of the horse's forgiving and tractable nature that he allows us to change his way of life completely and is still willing to do our bidding. We take him from his mother's side usually earlier than nature intended; we bring him in from the vast outdoors that is his natural environment and put him in a stable, and we reduce his intake of "Doctor Green" – grass, his natural food – and feed him oats and concentrates and feedstuffs he would never otherwise take. And still he wants to please us.

In domesticating the horse and adapting him to suit our needs, we are constantly shaping this marvellous animal to our ideal. Thoroughbred horses are bred to mature early and are prepared to race at two years old. And as increasingly sophisticated techniques are developed, such as artificial insemination using fresh, chilled or frozen semen – the latter can be shipped between continents so the stallion and mare never actually meet – the horse of today may well be unrecognizable another two thousand years hence.

Embryo transfer is used increasingly in sport horse breeding. An egg from a proven competition mare can be fertilized and implanted in a different broodmare who will develop and nurture the baby as her own while his biological mother can continue to compete. And in 2003 there were reports of the first cloned horse – now there is an idea to trifle with! Imagine twenty Desert Orchids or Miltons; if there was a race of fifteen Shergars, which one would win? To the purist, it is a conjecture of nightmare proportions.

Let us persevere in breeding wonderful, beautiful and talented equines and may they continue to reward our endeavors. But let us hope also that there will always be wild herds of horses who will evolve and thrive and flourish as nature intended.

> *"It is an endorsement of the horse's forgiving and tractable nature that he allows us to change his way of life completely and is still willing to do our bidding."*

Right: *Young Arabians show off their paces at the Royal Stables, Abu Dhabi*

Chapter 8

HEAVY HORSES

HEAVY HORSES

"He serves without servility, He has fought without enmity,
There is nothing so powerful, Nothing less violent..."
These words from a poem could have been written
specifically for the loyal heavy horse.

RONALD DUNCAN'S beautiful poem *The Horse* describes our noble steeds perfectly, but it is easy to forget that the world's heavy horse breeds were initially developed as warhorses. As British as the Bulldog, England's best-known heavy horse breed, the Shire, is spectacular; he can stand 18hh or even taller. Combining substance with quality, the Shire descended from the mediaeval warhorse, known as the Great Horse, who was renamed the English Black by Oliver Cromwell during England's brief history as a Commonwealth.

In the fourteenth century, one hundred stallions were brought over from Lombardy in northern Europe to be crossed with English native mares to breed a heavier, stronger horse. These were living armored tanks, initially developed to be sufficiently strong to bear a mediaeval knight in full armor and carrying weighty weapons, and still be agile enough to carry him into battle. The knight would only get on to his horse just before engaging in combat, and until then the horse was led from the right by the knight's squire.

Although strong, these horses were not as big as today's Shire and, as demand grew for a bigger, sturdier draft animal to work the land, the English Black was improved further by using Flanders or Flemish Horse blood from the Netherlands and, later, Friesian blood was introduced. Developed around the Midlands of England by the disciples of Robert Bakewell (1725-1795), the breed became known as the Bakewell Black. These horses were then crossed with Thoroughbreds for size and, as different colors began to appear, the "Black" became a misnomer and the breed was renamed the English Cart Horse in 1878.

The foundation stallion of the modern Shire is the Packington Blind Horse, who stood at Ashby-de-la-Zouche in Leicestershire in 1755-1770 and appears in the English Cart Horse Society's first studbook published in 1878. The breed organisation changed its name to the Shire Horse Society in 1884, the new name reflecting the breed's origins from the shire counties of the Midlands.

Diligent monitoring of the breed eliminated early soundness and wind problems and the horse became much in demand, both in Britain and the United States, which imported Shires with alacrity, the American Shire Horse Association being formed in 1885. The fortune of the Shire – and subsequently his value – rose, and his future seemed assured. During the Great Depression, good Shire foals were nicknamed "the rent-payers". However, with increasing mechanisation, the Shire almost became extinct after World War II – between 1947-1948, an estimated one hundred thousand were destroyed and the annual number of foals registered dwindled to eighty.

Left: *Originally known as the English Black, Shire horses take their name from the shire counties of England's Midlands where they were bred*

Previous pages: *The Shire, Britain's best-known heavy horse breed, still used to pull brewer's drays, has a noble head with a roman nose and a kind eye*

Above: *A Shire mare and foal pictured at the New England Shire Center in Florida, where the breed is very popular*

Left above and below: *Although immensely strong and powerful, the Shire has a kind nature – he has earned the title of "gentle giant"*

Thanks to dedicated breeders, the Shire Horse was saved from extinction and has enjoyed a revival in the past fifty years or so. And the breed is spectacular; the Shire can stand 18hh or even higher and combines substance with undeniable quality – Shires crossed with Thoroughbreds often make useful show-jumpers. His noble head, with its Roman (convex) nose, is long and lean, and his large, kind eye is full of intelligence.

The Shire has a comparatively long neck for a draft horse and a broad, powerful chest, deep girth, and short back, with well-muscled quarters. His clean, hard limbs have plenty of bone and abundant long, fine hair – known as feather – around the feet. There are still plenty of black Shires, a throwback perhaps to his early origins, but brown, bay, and grey are also common, with white markings. The society does not permit chestnut or roan in stallions, although the latter is acceptable in mares, which also tend to be a little smaller and more "feminine".

These gentle giants are still used, in some parts of the UK, to work the land and Shire classes at agricultural shows are among the most popular, while the breed has its own national show each spring at Peterborough in Cambridgeshire, England.

Above: *This fine stallion is beautifully proportioned with the breed's typically noble head*

Left: *This Shire mare shows the abundant fine feather of the breed*

"His noble head, with its Roman (convex) nose, is long and lean, and his large, kind eye is full of intelligence."

"The Clydesdale is described as having a flamboyant style, a flashy, spirited bearing and a high-stepping action."

I F THE Shire is a gentle giant, then his close cousin, the Clydesdale, is a scaled down version. Originating in the Clyde Valley region of Scotland, the Clydesdale – or Clydesman's Horse, as he was once known – developed from crossing hardy native stock with Flemish horses and, in the nineteenth century, infusions of Shire blood were introduced to further improve the breed.

Right: *The long-legged Clydesdale has very active paces and is singularly elegant among the draft breeds*

Above: *Bay, brown, grey, and black are common colors in the Clydesdale, although roans and piebalds, like this one, are sometimes seen*

Above left : *The Clydesdale is popular in the United States; these youngsters are pictured at a stud in Florida*

Left: *White patches on the face, legs and underbelly are common in the Clydesdale*

Following pages: *A Clydesdale mare and foal – the baby already has the beginnings of the fine feather on his legs*

Shire blood was introduced via Shire mares by two breeders, Lawrence Drew and David Liddell, who were convinced that the Clydesdale and the Shire were two branches of the same breed.

And, indeed, the two are very similar but, while the Clydesdale can certainly reach the same heights as the Shire, he is a lighter and more elegant breed, with noticeably longer legs; unusual in a draft horse. He has a finer, lighter head, too, with a straighter profile, and a longer neck. The average height is 16.2hh and he is renowned for his good limbs and hard, enduring feet.

In the first studbook of the Clydesdale Horse Society in 1878, he was described as having "a flamboyant style, a flashy, spirited bearing and a high-stepping action that makes him a singularly elegant animal among draft horses. "

The breed society was formed in 1877, with one thousand stallions listed in its first studbook. The American society followed a year later, where the breed is still popular, and the Clydesdale also earned the title of "the breed that built Australia". Sadly, he is yet another of Britain's native breeds that is listed by the Rare Breeds Survival Trust as "at risk".

Left: *A Suffolk Punch foal – every Suffolk Punch can be traced back to one stallion, Thomas Crisp's Horse Of Ufford*

Below: *A Suffolk Punch mare and her sturdy, upstanding foal*

Below right: *All Suffolk Punches are chesnut, correctly spelt without the first "t", and white markings are rare*

THE OXFORD English Dictionary, defines the word "punch" as a short-legged, thickset draft horse, a description that fits East Anglia's heavy horse breed perfectly. Every one is descended from one stallion, Thomas Crisp's Horse Of Ufford, foaled in 1768. The Suffolk Punch has the oldest breed society and the longest written pedigree of any heavy horse.

Suffolk Punches are always chesnut – correctly spelt without the first "t" when referring to this breed – and have no feather on their legs, which makes them well suited to working the heavy clay lands of East Anglia in the east of England. Standing between 16-16.2hh, he is a compact, robust horse, able to survive on meagre rations. He has a broad, noble head set on a thick powerful neck, and thick body, with powerful quarters. A roly-poly little horse, he is most attractive, but is sadly listed as "critical" by the Rare Breed Survival Trust.

"The Suffolk Punch has the longest written pedigree of any heavy horse."

BELGIUM IS justly proud of her heavy horse breed, the Brabant, or Belgian Heavy Draft. Formerly known as the Flanders horse, he has played a major part in the development of Britain's draft breeds, the Shire, Clydesdale, and Suffolk Punch, and was also instrumental in the Irish Draft (chapter 4), in which he was used to increase size.

The Brabant, and, by association the Ardennais, to whom he is closely related, was lauded by Julius Caesar as a strong and willing work horse. Over the years, the Belgians resisted the temptation to produce lighter horses for cavalry and jealously guarded their draft breed, who was ideal for working the land.

Toward the end of the nineteenth century, the breed – which was also sometimes referred to as the *race de trait Belge* – had developed into three main strains, based on separate bloodlines. These were Orange I, who was to found the Big Horse of Dendre line; Bayard, founder of Grey Horse of Nivelles line, who tended to throw red roan and sorrel

progeny, and Jean I, who founded the Colossal Horse of Mehaigne line, which is renowned for having great strength in the back and loins.

Red roans are still common, and are a throwback to the breed's primitive origins, as well as chestnut and sorrel, but bays, buckskins, and greys can also occur.

Fantastically strong and enduring, the Brabant is short-backed and compact, with short, sturdy legs with some feather. His head is quite fine and small for a heavy horse breed, although it remains in proportion. He averages about 17hh and is, overall, a massive creature. His action is far from elegant, being the typically choppy stride of the draft breeds, but it is ideally suited to working the land – especially heavy clay – and he is particularly known for his kind and willing temperament.

Although the Brabant is little known in Europe, he has found a following in the USA, where he has been bred to be more refined and stylish.

Left: *For a draft breed, the Brabant has a comparatively fine, small head*

Right: *The Brabant, or Belgian Heavy Draft, is a massive, powerful horse with a kind and willing temperament*

Left: *A Brabant mare and foal, pictured in their native Belgium, where the breed was developed to work the heavy clay soil*

*"The Brabant was
lauded by Julius Caesar as a strong and
willing work horse."*

Left and above: *This Brabant mare is a lovely example of the breed
and has the sorrel coloring with flaxen mane and tail that is
common. She is pictured at a stud in Texas, the breed being
particularly popular in the United States*

HOLLAND'S HEAVY horse, the Dutch Draft, is a comparatively new breed, having been developed in 1918 from the Brabant, Belgian's draft breed. He is a massive horse and phenomenally strong – he was intended as an agricultural breed and his strength is essential for working the heavy clay and sandy soil of the Netherlands, which would tire out lesser horses.

He is an intelligent creature and has a kind, willing nature. Standing just under 17hh, he is surprisingly active for his size and, because he has a long working life and is a "good doer", he is an economical equine to keep. In looks, he is similar to the Brabant and also resembles the Belgian Ardennais, some of which were used as outcrosses when establishing the breed. Although he is of massive build, his head should not be too coarse and his kind eye indicates his gentle temperament.

He has a short neck, powerful shoulders, and a wide, strong back. His tail is set low on muscular quarters and his short, sturdy legs have plenty of black feather. He is generally chestnut, bay, grey or roan.

Above: *The Dutch Draft is a massively built, powerful horse with a kind temperament and willing nature*

Above right: *A distinctive characteristic of the Dutch Draft is his generous black feather*

Right: *This Dutch Draft foal already has the powerful, short neck of the breed*

Above left and right: *The Percheron has a distinctive and stylish action, with long, low and free paces*

Left: *Percherons are popular worldwide, having been exported to Canada, Usa, Australia, South Africa, and Japan*

UNLIKELY AS it may seem in a draft horse breed, Arabian blood has played a major part in the development of the Percheron. Horses almost certainly existed in the Perche region – from which the breed takes its name – of Normandy since the Ice Age and it is thought that eastern blood was introduced after the first Crusade at the end of the eleventh century.

The renowned Le Pin stud, the principal breeding center for Percherons, imported Arabian stallions in 1760 as outcrosses and two of those, Godolphin and Gallipoly, proved influential. Because of the Arabian influence, the Percheron is perhaps the most elegant of heavy horse breeds, with the eastern blood particularly noticeable in the fine, slightly concave head. Typically, the Percheron is grey – an Arabian color – or sometimes black and he has a distinctive long and low action.

He is one of the biggest breeds of heavy horse – indeed, the world's largest horse, Dr Le Gear, was a Percheron, standing an impressive 21hh!

"The Percheron is the most elegant of the heavy horse breeds, due to Arabian influences."

Left: *Typically, the Percheron is grey – an Arabian color – or black*

Right: *Arabian influences can be seen in the Percheron's fine, elegant head*

Glossary

airs above the ground movements of the high school, or
Haute École, in which the horse's forelegs, or forelegs and
hindlegs leave the ground

bloodstock Thoroughbred horses

breed specific equine group with particular characteristics

coldblood generic name for draft or heavy horses

coffin head coarse, plain head

colt uncastrated male horse under the age of four

cover mating a stallion and a mare

dam the mother of a foal

dished face concave, like that of the Arabian

dorsal or eel stripe a darker line running along the spine
from the wither to the croup, most commonly seen on a
buckskin coat

ewe neck a conformation fault in which the neck appears to
be set on 'backward'

feather long silky hair on the lower leg most often seen on
heavy horses and some pony breeds

feral an animal that was once domesticated but has since
been released or has escaped back into the wild, or
another term for wild

filly a female horse under the age of four

foal a young horse up to the age of twelve months

gelding castrated male horse

good doer a horse which thrives on a minimum amount of food

hands the unit of measurement for horses, often abbreviated
to hh for "hands high". A hand is four inches or 102mm

high school or *Haute École* – see airs above the ground

high-set tail the tail is set high on the quarters

hotblood either an Arab or a Thoroughbred horse

mare female horse over the age of four

nick division and resetting of the muscles under the tail to
affect a high carriage

outcross using blood from a different breed to refine or
develop another breed

piebald a horse which is black and white in color

poll the area of the top of the head between the ears

roach back conformation fault, where the curve of the
horse's back is convex rather than concave

Roman nose convex profile of the head

sclera the white outer membrane of the eyeball as seen in
the Appaloosa

skewbald a horse that is white with patches of any other
color, except black (see piebald)

stallion uncastrated male horse over the age of four

studbook register kept by a breed society to record pedigrees
of pure stock

warmblood in general terms, horses that are crosses of both
hotblood, such as the Arabian, and coldblood, such as the
draft breeds